THE MAGGOT PEOPLE

THE MAGGOT PEOPLE

a novel

Henning Koch

DZANC
BOOKS

DZANC
BOOKS

5220 Dexter Ann Arbor Rd.
Ann Arbor, MI 48103
www.dzancbooks.org

Published 2014 by Dzanc Books
ISBN: 978-1938103537
First edition: November 2014

This project is supported in part by the National Endowment for
the Arts and the MCACA.

Printed in the United States of America

10   9   8   7   6   5   4   3   2   1

I see myself again, my skin pitted by mud and pestilence, my hair and armpits full of worms, and even bigger worms in my heart, lying among strangers without age, without feeling...

—Rimbaud, *A Season in Hell*

... And Jesus hurt me when he deserted me but I have forgiven you Jesus for giving me all this love when there is no one I can turn to in this world...

—Morrissey, *I Have Forgiven Jesus*

Michael

1.

At the age of twenty-three, Michael had the bad fortune to inherit his grandmother's house in the south of France. For two long years, he spent his time dutifully going to the bar, buying drinks for strangers and talking about topics such as partridge shooting and viticulture, neither of which interested him very much. There was something fundamentally hopeless about his attempt to cultivate a local outlook in Provence. A typical local man in Michael's village home was a cardigan-wearing inhabitant in his sixties, passionate about using his body as a sort of temporary wine barrel. Michael struggled for human companionship and felt like the oddest man in the world.

Back in Finsbury Park, London, where he used to live in a rented room, Michael had never done much more than play backgammon and drink Red Stripe with his neighbor, an unemployed drummer. Occasionally, when his anxious mother had called to tell Michael that he had to find himself a job, he almost gloatingly told her his favorite words of wisdom: "Consider the lilies of the field, mum. They don't work, do they?"

Since coming to France, Michael no longer had the benefits of Social Security or a like-minded neighbour. He tried all sorts of activities to brighten up his existence and earn him a living of some kind. At first he thought he'd have a go at carpentry. After spending weeks laying a new floor upstairs (to stop himself crashing through the rotten floorboards), he found to his annoyance that the cheap pine boards warped in the humidity and creaked underfoot like dissatisfied old men. Later he got hold of a decrepit car which he thought he might use to familiarize himself with mechanics. He spent days scrutinizing a manual before deciding that his hands were not made to mess about with screwdrivers and socket sets. It led only to temper fits, oily lacerations, and a mad desire to commit arson.

Clearly, if he was to have a job of some kind, it would have to be rooted in the creative industries, as they were known.

Among the jumble of the attic he'd found a large easel and a box of spattered tubes of oil paints. It seemed an invitation, but as he was coming very late to the art of painting, his technical abilities were limited.

His first attempt was a family portrait based on a memory of himself and his father on a beach in Normandy while his mother sat under a bright parasol waving at them. In the end the technical problems of this emotive subject proved too much for him. Instead he went back to his usual motif, which he'd been scribbling in the margins of his school notebooks since he was eleven or twelve. Michael could not quite explain his liking for the walled city he always depicted clinging to the sides of a rocky pinnacle, more or less like Tolkien's *Minas Tirith* or Mann's monastery in *The Magic Mountain*. He assumed it was something obsessive that always brought him back to the same rocks and crags—the air filled with philosophical eagles spreading their wings and casting noble glances at the human fortifications below.

He began to worry that his mind was dissolving. At night he'd wake and lie hyperventilating. A few times he went jogging through the dark village, pursued by outraged hounds. He sat by the mountain painting, which seemed to settle his nerves. He napped in his chair, a blanket round his shoulders, or just listened to the dormant house and the night passing.

His churning question was always the same: *What am I doing here? What am I trying to achieve?*

And so, almost twenty-six months into his French sojourn, Michael still had not found out what he was supposed to be doing with his life.

Back in England, his parents had recently passed away when a derailed train came hurtling through their house just as they were settling in with their tea tray—the bulbous China pot under its custom-made chicken cozy, two chocolate digestives each, and oranges—to watch the six o'clock news. Before they knew it, they had *fused* with the country's news offering, which would particularly have pleased Michael's father, who was interested in domestic politics, although of course they never had the pleasure of seeing themselves on television.

Michael took a ferry back to England from Le Havre. It was a misty morning. The oily waters of the Channel lapped against the stinking hull of the giant ship. The fabled white cliffs of Dover materialized like large stage backdrops to an operetta. He felt obliged to cry, but a terrible sense of unreality made him doubt the impulse. Standing there on deck, he brooded as he watched his native country coming into view through the haze.

Michael now had two houses, or rather, he had one house in Provence and another in Borehamwood with a large train on top of it. Luckily the emergency services took the view that it was their responsibility to remove it, which was a good thing. Michael spent a day sifting through the rubble, but it's amazing how efficiently a burning train pulverizes a human dwelling. The solidity of buildings is really a bit of a sham. Solidity is illusory. The universe is constructed from tiny fragments that have a tendency to pulverize when struck by a great force, he mockingly told himself as he wandered about at the bottom of the garden, where a few daffodils were doing their best to maintain a semblance of normality. Wedged into a rhododendron bush, Michael found a smashed chest, from which blackened cutlery had spilled. Inside were some neatly pressed tablecloths and a couple of oven gloves, which he later brought back to France but could not quite bring himself to use. Should they be framed, perhaps, as a sort of keepsake?

At the end of that heavy day in Borehamwood, he decided to knock back a couple of shots of whiskey before returning to London. As soon as he stepped into the pub, he was able to confirm to himself that Borehamwood was quite likely even duller than Provence, although there were more similarities than one might have thought. In Borehamwood, men in beige or brown corduroy trousers drank flat, hop-stinking beer. Women opted for shapeless skirts slung around their hips like loincloths. Vaguely menacing younger women wore sharp heels strapped to their feet. They drank a kind of white wine that the French might have described as a soda pop.

Also, the English diet had an element of the humdrum about it: baked beans, fried eggs and bacon were interspersed with fish fingers, liver and onions, or pork sausages spattered with punishingly strong mustard. On Sundays, English people had a custom of consulting glossy cookery books, then resignedly putting large cuts of meat in the oven and watching cricket matches while the house filled with carbonized smog. Instead of viticulture they liked to talk about how many pheasants or rabbits they'd shot. In England there was more interest in the actual shooting part, whereas Frenchmen hunted for the pot.

If he ever did go back to England, the government would very likely enroll him on some plebeian course in Modern Morality and Citizenship Standards for the 21st Century. English politicians were brilliant at coming up with these types of schemes. When they first applied to enter Parliament, they had to be able to show gnomish or dwarven ancestry. This was a requirement of public service—it was believed, quite correctly, that only gnomes had the necessary oddness and fondness for gold to be able to represent their sceptred isle.

At least in France no one bothered with you. Especially if you were foreign they considered you an irrelevance and this was much better.

In any case the possibilities of going back to England were scuppered by a long, flowery letter from an insurance company, explaining that because of his parents' invalid insurance policy, there would be no payout on their house. Soon after, a carefully worded letter from the train company expressed sincere regret about flattening his family, then offered a very small amount of statutory compensation.

"Engineering, that's a good subject," his father had once advised Michael when the question of his education came up. "An engineer is never out of work." How uncanny that, in the end, a group of plotting engineers got together, built a train, laid some tracks by his house and maliciously finished him off one evening just as the poor man was looking forward to his cup of tea.

After Michael had gone back to Provence, the electrics in the house started playing up and he worried he'd have to find the money to rewire the place. His bedroom became a particular problem. In its earlier days, the house had been used as a residence for seminarians—young virginal men preparing for ordination, narrowly preferred in those times to a life of digging the sod. He often saw a ghostly figure at night, floating across the room to fiddle with his bedroom ceiling light. As a result, Michael had to change the lightbulb every few days. It irritated him. Was he not entitled to live in a house that had been the legal property of his grandmother, a respectable French woman who had bought the house fair and square at a church auction? Nowadays it was little more than an emanation of humidity and mold. Surely the spirits should be happy that someone was willing to live there at all?

The ghost problem got pervasive enough for Michael to seek advice about it. He went to Alain, the retired village priest, a tiny stooped man with poetical eyes and silvered temples. His grandmother had once been very fond of him; she used to sweep his church for him and polish the candlesticks.

Alain nodded knowingly and tapped the side of his nostril, then whipped out a bunch of dried herbs, set fire to them, and spent the morning walking round Michael's house, waving the smoke about whilst intoning prayers.

"That should do it," he said, reposing in one of grandmother's toxic armchairs. "It's nothing to worry about."

"Well, I am worried about it. I seem to be having terrible luck."

"It's not about luck," said Alain. "This spirit is angry with you for not being a Catholic and for soiling the house with your disrespect. I take it you're abusing yourself?"

"I don't really see what business of his it is," said Michael. "People don't choose their religion. Some are born in Salt Lake City and they can't do anything about it."

Alain did not understand Michael's comment and put it down to the young man's confusion. Gently he put his knobbly hand on Michael's sleeve and said, with a sage nod, as if what he was about to suggest was in some way revolutionary:

"You're an orphan now, my boy. What you need is to get married... to a nice girl... who does not have the Devil in her eyes."

After Alain had gone, Michael went to the kitchen, a sort of studio and storage area for junk. He sat there sipping his morning coffee, whilst staring at the big canvas of the mountain, trying to assess how he could improve it. Seized by a notion, he painted a small figure in one of the windows: a woman leaning out, hanging up a garment on a clothesline. As soon as she was there—a tiny black smudge in a corner—he felt she had acquired a life of her own. But who was she? What was she doing in that city among the tiered rooftops? And did she have the Devil in her eyes?

Somehow he felt he might prefer her if she did.

2.

Waking up in the old house had a certain ceremoniousness to it. He lay there listening, feeling himself enclosed as if in a tomb, the shutters excluding every bit of light; yet by the distracted sound of birds idly twittering under the tiles or the whoosh and scrape of incoming swifts, he knew it was morning.

Eventually he got up and, after stepping into a pair of threadbare slippers, dragged himself across the rough stone floor to the window. Opening the shutters was one of the great perks of Provence. The sky, always blue and pristine, surprised him every morning. There was something marvelous about existing on the inside of this bright, oxygenated bell.

In the street he heard mothers scolding their children, also the slamming of pots in kitchens and mouthwatering smells of meat or shellfish being cooked in oil and garlic. When he saw the vivid sky overhead, he had a sense of life happening around him—his place in it more or less that of the alien or automaton, concerned with drinking his coffee, lighting his cigarette, munching his dry bread and cheese and then shuffling off to expel his bodily waste.

There was a measure of humiliation to the whole thing, he thought to himself, sitting there on the cracked seat beneath the sputtering cistern. "I am not an animal, but all I ever seem to do is eat, drink, and shit."

Whilst indulging in his usual self-flagellation, he saw a large seagull landing on the roof opposite. Flat-footed, it made its way to a crack in the tiles, stuck its beak inside and pulled out a fluffy nestling, then tipped its head back and tossed the little flapping thing down its gullet. All round its head, swifts were darting, screaming, performing aerial displays, zigzagging between chimney pots and clotheslines—fully engaged in the pressing duty of procreation. Very well, they seemed to be saying, we have lost one but we can make another. It was a good Catholic view.

Downstairs in the kitchen, the dripping tap nagged at the piles of crockery left from last night. He had an espresso with plenty of sugar and added his empty coffee cup to the greasy mound in the sink.

After showering under a tepid, limp spout of water that emerged with a vibrating humming sound, like an aged diesel engine, Michael dressed and went out to have breakfast. He stopped in front of the painting and cast another beady eye on the woman in the window.

Possibly because his mind was already on the subject, he was more receptive when he saw the girl crossing the square. A primitive mechanism was set off in his brain. He knew he was powerless to resist because he was the mechanism, he actually heard it groaning into life and felt the emergence of the foolish love cliché, like a cuckoo springing out of its clock.

He stood, one arm extended as if he were a blind man trying to stop himself crashing into a wall.

The girl had also stopped and was facing him with a complex frown on her face.

Between them, in the village square, there was a good deal of bustle. Parents drove their herds of infants across the concrete with much cracking of their whips and loud cries. A group of Chilean immigrants had set up market stalls in a corner, hawking the meat grinders, flour sifters, rolling pins and other historical artifacts that they filched from dying widows and sold to tourists. Chinese merchants were also piling up their defective wares.

Michael was surprised when she steered her steps towards him, threading her way through the busy square until she stood in front of him. He brought his arm down—it seemed the right thing to do.

"I noticed you were watching me," she said,

"Was I?"

"I was just wondering why?" said the girl, and as she spoke he noticed one of her side incisors jutting out. There was something owlish about it, like a tiny beak; he half-expected seeing a mouse tail hanging out, the remnants of her last meal.

"I don't know. I noticed you, that's all," he said awkwardly.

"Well, if you're sure."

She turned round and started walking away at a good pace. With her back turned, he had an excellent opportunity to look at her some more. She was wearing espadrilles and a dark strapless dress that showed off her smooth limbs.

She stopped at one of the non-Chilean, non-Chinese stalls to buy eggplants and grapes and pack them into her cloth bag.

Within a matter of hours, the locals were aware of the presence of a tourist who must have rented somewhere to stay nearby—yet another of these puzzling individuals carrying plenty of money and wandering about in search of something. No one knew who she was, nor did it particularly matter; although, in a village, such things are considered important.

Michael began to keep tabs on her, though more carefully, to avoid detection. Next time they spoke, he felt, it had to be more purposeful and not so foolish.

She crossed the square every morning at nine o'clock precisely and this suited him perfectly. It gave him time for ablutions and coffee. Sometimes he followed her and sometimes watched her in the distance.

A few times he saw her sitting motionless and amphibious in the sun, a pair of oversize sunglasses obscuring most of her face.

When he learned where she was staying, it made perfect sense: a scruffy bungalow by the beach with a fence of old car doors, prickly pear trees, and rusting bed frames lashed together with wire. The place had been abandoned for years and lay shuttered and steeped in silence, its overgrown garden populated by stray cats drawn by the fish she put out for them and left to go putrid in the sun. Burgeoning fig trees pressed against the walls, plunging the front entrance in welcome shade. He never saw anyone sitting on the rusty cast-iron chairs by the table on the patio.

In the drive was a beaten-up Ford Transit with Spanish plates. He assumed it had to be hers.

Many times he followed her to the edge of the dunes, then stopped and watched her scaling the sandy mounds, the cloth bag slung over her shoulder. He always stopped in the shadow at the edge of the trees and let her merge with the yellows and browns of the blowing sands.

She never looked back.

3.

One day he found himself sitting on the beach just below her house. The cicadas were scraping monotonously. He was stupefied; he'd been there an hour or more when the gate screeched and he saw her coming in a very straight line towards him, stopping at a distance of about ten paces.

With her hands on her hips, she called out in a flustered voice: "I know you like me, but why do you have to follow me all the time?"

It was a fair question. He stood up and said, defensively: "I'm only sitting on the beach. I think I'm entitled to sit here. It's not your beach, is it?"

"Every morning I wake up, I open the door and I see you sitting right there. Or I go to the village. And what do I see?" She moved a little closer. "I see you, I see your face; your big eyes watching me."

Michael felt caught out; he had to come up with something convincing. "I think I'm just bored. I'm not from here; I'm from England. People here don't like me. They think I'm just a foreigner... and I am a foreigner."

She laughed and the sound of her voice carried across the sands, reaching the ears of the other bathers who seemed to accept Michael's presence more readily now that a lovely owl-faced girl was laughing with him.

She tilted her head and judged him, which made him feel much better. No one had judged him in a long time, at least no one with warm eyes. "So you're following me and you admit it. Don't you have anything better to do with your time?"

"Being busy is overrated. People who know what they're doing don't do a bloody thing."

"Even something nice like having an ice cream?"

"That's different."

Her name was Ariel; her hand was cool and dry. They went back to the house, where a big Alsatian was sitting very neatly on the porch with its paws together.

"Give me ten minutes," she said.

"Does he bite?"

"Only if you bite him first."

She went inside and closed the door.

The dog gave him a heartbroken look and sighed deeply. Michael sat down on the step and muttered under his breath: "I know how you feel."

From somewhere—maybe inside his head or carried by the wind? —he heard the dog's reply: "Go home, never speak to her again, she doesn't belong to herself, she's property. I'm property, too. Do you understand?" Then, with another sigh, the dog added: "Oh Lord, how could he understand?"

When he looked at the Alsatian, it was sitting there in what broadly speaking he would describe as a doglike manner, its long pink tongue on its massive teeth.

Ariel came back wearing a short camouflage-print dress that showed her softly muscular legs and well-formed hips—her skin was like an almond kernel under the husk, polished and smooth.

They walked down a sun-dappled path under Mediterranean pines and Michael tried to recompose himself.

Ariel didn't waste time. "So you're bored, are you? That's such a waste; don't you have family here? A wife? Girlfriend?"

"No. My folks passed away. I only came here because my grandmother left me her house."

"So you decided to live here, in this little shriveled anus. Correct me if I'm wrong, but just because someone leaves you a house doesn't mean you have to live in it. Right?"

He laughed, slightly forced. "I don't really *live* here…"

"Sorry, but you do, you know."

What about you? What are you doing here, he thought to himself. How did you end up here?

Ariel glanced at him. "I'm convalescing. That's what I'm doing here."

"You've been unwell?"

She nodded. "I had a breakdown, I lost the will to get up in the mornings. Have you ever had that? One day I just decided to die. I lay there like a lump for a month without moving. I didn't eat for two whole months. I was on hunger strike. Just the odd mouthful of water."

"Hunger strike against what?" He tried to smile: "You're not being serious, are you?"

"So I made myself get up," she said, ignoring his question. "I drove down here and found this house. I thought I'd get some sea air and straighten myself out."

"This is the last place I'd come if I wanted to straighten myself out."

"Places don't straighten people out. It's the other way round," said Ariel.

He did not quite understand what she meant. There was a rush of excitement bubbling through him, the mere thought that all this might soon be *his*. Soon he would touch that overwhelming presence: woman, like a valley with green slopes and a stream flowing through the center. When he looked at her, she seemed less excited about it all: she wore a sort of peeved expression as if life was an inconvenience to her.

By now they'd reached the hinterland of the village. Walking up the main street towards the square, they seemed to be forcing their way through a tangle of staring eyes. A group of builders outside the wine cooperative elbowed each other and winked knowingly. Ever since Ariel's arrival they had been sharpening their knives, assessing and weighing up her thighs, buttocks, and breasts as if she were a Christmas sow. The two old madams in the ice cream shop stared at them with their usual bleak disapproval and horror.

Outside, Michael tried not to look as Ariel licked her ice cream.

"Michael. I'm nothing special, you know, so don't start fantasizing about me. I've had a hard life. I've got nothing to show for it except a rusty old van, a dysfunctional dog, and nowhere to go."

"Will you come back? Have lunch with me?"

"Where do you live?"

"There." Michael pointed to a big gray stone house across the square.

"Oh, God… looks like an old hornet's nest."

"There's one only hornet left now, and he's lost his sting," said Michael.

They crossed the emptying lunchtime square, bathed in strong, liquid light. Michael led her into his front yard, past the rusty car, through a stand of nettles growing in calcified manure. The house had a kind of infested charm. If you could ignore the years of neglect (but you couldn't) and if you could forget about the smell of depression (but you couldn't), it was really a quaint old charming house deep in Provence where nothing—not even time—would ever change anything.

He called out over his shoulder: "I've been here a few years, can't think where else to go."

She strode ahead of him into the house. He directed her into the kitchen and decided not to take her upstairs to show her the sad warren of neglected bedrooms with sunken beds, soggy plaster, and water-stained prints of the Madonna.

Ariel stopped in front of the painting of the mountain. "This I like," she said and seemed relieved that she had found one thing that pleased her. She pointed, finding the tiny smudge of the girl in the window, leaning out to fix something to the washing line. "I like the girl. I'd like to know her name."

"Why?"

"Because otherwise she's just a figment of your imagination. Do you mind if we eat on the porch? In case I need to leave in a hurry."

He knocked up some *vichyssoise*, which they had cold with crisp white wine and fresh bread with a good strong goat's cheese. They sat on the stone steps and ate in silence. He was uncomfortable: even a monosyllabic exchange seemed beyond him.

Ariel put down her half-finished plate and stretched. "Delicious. And don't worry about not speaking. It's utterly overrated, this constant pitter-patter of words. Drives you nuts. Most of it doesn't even mean anything. It's fear."

Michael thought about putting on some music, but once again she seemed to have an eerie ability to preempt him. "Listening to Leonard Cohen in a haunted house can drive a person to suicide. Especially *Avalanche*."

"I always listen to Leonard Cohen. I *love* that song."

"That's what I mean." She stood up. "I always find there's something sinister about other people's houses. Let's go to my place?"

"Your house is far more sinister than mine."

"Subjectivity will be the death of us."

4.

They made their way through the narrow streets past the church immodestly covered in threadbare stucco and across the main highway with a sprinkling of traffic in the early afternoon sun. With relief they put civilization behind them and took the sandy track through the pine woods to the dunes and the ever-fresh sea.

By the time they stopped he had broken into a sweat.

Ariel was cool as porcelain in his hands but she wriggled out of his grip.

"You're fast; that's good. I mean I've known *faster*, but you're not bad," she said, slightly flustered.

"You're quite fast yourself."

"Waiting is pointless. Pursuit is also pointless."

Below her bungalow, intrepid bathers had put up parasols on the blinding white beach. A few of them were standing in the water, partially submerged, mostly looking out to the horizon as if puzzled by this expanse that stood in their way.

Ariel ran into the sea, diving athletically into a wave. He followed her and caught up with her under the water. Her skin had a lubricated quality a little like a dolphin, he imagined. They kissed fleetingly as they surfaced, but again she pulled away.

"All right, then," she said, slightly wearied by foregone conclusions. "Shall we go back to my place?"

Without waiting for his answer, she waded back.

———————

Inside the beach house it was dark as pitch. Ariel fumbled for a dusty floor-lamp and turned it on.

"Wouldn't it be easier to pull up a shutter?"

"They're nailed down."

Michael scanned the place, but there wasn't much to see. Cheap composite furniture. A bookcase empty but for a dusty Bible, a conch shell inscribed with the name "Santiago" in red ink, and a mangy, stuffed bee-eater with a plastic maggot in its beak.

Ariel followed his eyes. "I like that bird a lot; he's got style," she said.

She filled the espresso maker and they went outside to sit at the rusty metal table under the fruit trees. Dusk was setting in.

She disappeared briefly round the corner, returning with a hammock dragging along the ground behind her like a huge dead octopus. After hooking it onto two ready-made fastenings round the trees, she fetched the coffee spluttering angrily from inside the house and lay down in the hammock whilst balancing her cup in her hand. Michael climbed in beside her.

"I feel bad about this," said Ariel. "I ought to make you a sandwich and send you home. Not because I don't like you; I do like you. But it might be better for you if you just stay clear of me."

He frowned: "Why, what's wrong with you?"

"I'm bad news. At least I'm honest about it. Some people pretend they're good but they're just waiting for the opportunity to bury a knife in your spine!"

They kissed for a while, until they heard the gruff, depressive voice of the Alsatian, still slumped under the metal table: "Ariel, just get this over with, will you? So we can go to Rome and get back to normal."

Ariel lifted her head: "You're such a conformist; I suppose it's your Austrian nature coming out. Let me ask you something,

Günter. You think I've got nothing better to do than spend my time sleeping in a box?"

"Who's asking for your opinion?" said the dog.

Michael came close to a nervous attack but he controlled himself.

Ariel got up abruptly and went inside.

He lay there for a while after she had gone, staring at the dark entrance, an angular slit cut into the white façade. He had to take a deep breath before crossing the threshold.

She was in the bedroom by the window where the blind was slightly raised, allowing a smidgeon of light to come through.

"We don't have much time," she said. "I never stay anywhere longer than a month. People are trying to find me and I don't want them to."

He looked at her, uneasy again. "Who?"

"Oh, a lot of thugs with a horrible attitude."

"Criminals?"

"No, *brutes*. My life is a nightmare, Michael. Either it's brutes hunting me down or pedants boring me to death."

Struggling with his confusion, he lunged forward. In an instant they'd fallen back into the bed, Ariel with her back to him, and he pushing into her with slow, circling movements. She pressed her strangely cool body against his. He could not have pulled away even if he'd wanted to, so intense was her gravitation. Yet he also had a weird notion that Ariel was releasing her essence into him—a sort of reversion. Where this thought came from he did not know; it disturbed him greatly.

"Thank you," he groaned into her ear, flooding with huge relief as he felt himself being released.

"For what?" she said, lying on her stomach and resting her head on his chest. "You fool; you rabbit fool. Why don't you put your feet on the ground? Breathe."

Again he noted her coolness. He touched her skin, amazed at her prodigious energy.

"You're right," he said. "I have to get out of here. I have to stop playing the fool."

"Don't. I like them," she said, adding a sleepy afterthought: "I don't like rabbits much, though." She paused. "You can come with us if you like. We're leaving for Switzerland. We know someone up there, she'll take care of us."

Possibly he slept for a while. He was unsure what the time was; his watch had no luminous dials and the room was so dark that only by closing his eyes could he ward off a sense of panic. Even the air was a dusty maelstrom reluctantly drawn into one's lungs.

"Oh good, you're back," Ariel whispered. "I had a dream: you and me were standing on a mountain looking down on a huge city. It filled the whole valley; there were roads and lights and buildings climbing almost the whole way up to the summit. Then a wave washed in from the sea. At first I thought, oh look, what a big wave. But it kept growing. It picked things up and carried them away. Boats, cars, buildings. People as well; they linked arms in the water and they were singing as the waters carried them along. The water kept rising, one couldn't see anything except the water rising. It was sliding by at an incredible speed. I remember there were clouds overhead also passing quite swiftly across the sky, but in the opposite direction. It was a frightening illusion; I mean it wasn't really an illusion, it was actually happening. All the earth and sky were just water and air rushing by while we stood there on a tiny piece of rock. I kept wanting to climb higher, but you kept touching my arm and telling me there was nowhere higher than this, there was nowhere else to climb to. The water was tugging at our ankles. I was terrified. Then it started receding; there was nothing left beneath. As it sank away I only saw black earth, bare wet earth with nothing alive on it, not so much as an earthworm wriggling or a fish left in a hollow; there weren't even any hollows or rocks. Everything was swept clean."

"Then what happened?"

5.

When he woke, a limpid sea breeze had cooled the land. A big crustaceous moon was cranking itself up from behind the dunes, appearing momentarily in the gap of the broken blind. He raised himself onto his elbow to look at Ariel, who was sleeping deeply. Her body seemed to be churning from inside, as if having an epileptic seizure. Muscles under her skin were tensing, rippling across her face and body in tight spasms.

He watched for a while, wondering what he should do.

Without warning, the seizure stopped and she opened her eyes and said, very brightly: "Oh, what a lovely sleep."

"What was that? Are you epileptic or something?"

"Don't worry; it's normal. It only happens at night."

"It looked painful." He paused, then added: "It never happened to me, that's for sure."

"How can you know?" she said, with a smile. "I mean… if you're asleep?" She lit a candle and sat there in silence, scrutinizing him again. "Can I tell you something? Your health isn't as good as you think. You have a small tumor growing on your liver."

"Any other defects?"

"I'm quite serious. You should listen to me."

"All women say that."

"I'm not really a woman in the proper sense of the word."

"I don't know how you can say that."

"No. You don't."

A few big breakers came in; he heard them churning against the sandbar. The sound was ominous—the distant music of a dream where anything could happen.

"Yesterday," said Ariel, "when I asked you to take me for an ice cream, I thought I'd give you the chance of deciding what you really thought of me."

"I knew that before we even spoke."

"I wouldn't have minded if you didn't like me. I'm not petty like that. If people don't like me, that's up to them."

He shrugged, slightly puzzled, then put his arm round her as if to reassure her. She snuggled close and they slept until sunrise. But as soon as he opened his eyes, the conversation continued where it had left off. Ariel was already there, waiting for him.

"You're one of us now. You do realize that?" she whispered.

"One of who?"

"Last night when I said your world would change, I really meant it. Literally. It's changed already. As I was saying, there's a tumor on your liver. You probably wouldn't have noticed it for another eight or nine months. By then it would have been too late, cancers are very aggressive nowadays. Humans are poisoning their world and they don't realize they are also poisoning themselves. Anyway. By this time next week the tumor will be gone. In fact, you won't have a liver at all."

Michael felt himself grow heavy as he looked at Ariel, her soft intimate eyes, her tumbling hair spilling over her shoulders.

"Oh, dear God," he said, sitting up abruptly. "I've been such an idiot."

"Why?"

He looked at her. "I'm going to tell you the story of my family. Okay? It's a very sad story so I'll keep it short. Dwelling on it won't improve things, I mean. Are you ready?"

"Yes."

"Suicide. Arsenic. Disinheritance. Obsession with money. Financial ruin. Broken hearts. Mad people spreading unhappiness all round them."

"Sounds like any other family to me," said Ariel chirpily. "And? What's your point?"

"And I want to finish with the whole thing. That's all."

Smooth as a snake, she sat up, slowly uncoiling her limbs and eyeing him with an expanding smile as if she meant to swallow him whole. He thought: you're the most beautiful girl I've ever seen, but you're mad, mad, mad. And I should have seen it; I should have avoided it!

"I'm not mad," she said.

Michael got out of bed and started getting dressed.

Ariel was watching him, her face analytical. "As you're leaving anyway, I'll tell you."

His movements grew hasty; he fiddled with his socks, desperate to be gone. She launched into her personal myth. "Because we've slept together, you're going to turn into someone like me. A maggot person."

He gave her a tense grin. "My God, Ariel," he said. "What's a *maggot person*?"

"It's someone whose body has been taken over by maggots. Invaded and conquered. The maggots eat your organs, they take over the functions of those organs, and they're much more efficient than you ever were. They eat everything in your body. The only thing they don't touch is your brain. You may find this unbelievable, but I'm actually solid maggot." She stood up in the bed, quite naked, and twirled for him, like a ballerina.

With resignation, Michael said: "Who would ever have thought it?"

"My dear man, you can pity me but later you'll know I was telling you the truth all along." She glared, then continued: "There's even a group of specialized maggots that eat your bones and form a hard core inside the rest of the maggots. The maggots pass oxygen to your brain. The maggots synchronize their movements, they work like muscles so you can walk and do whatever you like. Some of the best athletes in the world are actually maggots. People call it doping, but it's actually just maggots. Remember that World Cup final when Cristiano Ronaldo went strange? He was just having a few problems with his maggots. You see?"

"Aha." He was lacing up his shoes now.

"You know when you saw my skin churning?"

"Yes."

"That's when the maggots change places so they can all have some of the food a person has eaten."

"Okay."

"The maggots control all your bodily functions. Only about once a week will you need to excrete any waste products. And it will be a very small amount. Like bird droppings."

"Look, Ariel. I'm so sorry. But I'm going now."

"You're going to miss me terribly, because from now on you won't be like other people. In about a week you'll start realizing the maggots are taking over your body. You'll be in a lot of pain and no painkillers will be of any use because the maggots will eat the painkillers."

Panicked, he moved towards the door, but she followed him.

"Just for your sake I will stay here another ten days. Ten days, Michael. But don't tell anyone, especially *not* your doctor. If you do, and I think it's possible you will, you mustn't mention me at all, or they'll come here looking for me. In fact, your doctor will call the authorities if he realizes you're a maggot person."

He touched her arm. "I'll come and see you."

"I'm taking a big risk telling you all this. Most of my kind would just clear off now. But I'm not like them."

He stepped out of the door into the slanted, early-morning sunlight. The mistral was blowing, and he watched the frothy sea rolling in. He breathed deep, steered his steps back through

the sandy, grassy pine woods along the rutted track where people took their four-wheel-drives down to the dunes in summer.

He took one last look at the house, where she was still standing by the gate, her hair blowing in the wind, then shook his
head to be rid of her.

6.

A few times in the days that followed he made his way to the dunes and lay in the sand behind a tuft of sea grass, with his binoculars trained on the house—like a regular psychopath. Nothing ever moved there. Just once he saw the Alsatian emerge and flop down on the front step. Minutes later Ariel came out with a morning coffee and sat down beside him. They stared out at the sea, a sort of deep moroseness hanging over them.

At the sight of her face so far away, he found himself missing her; all that caustic wit and energy of hers, wasted on a sourpuss dog when she might have used it to much better effect on him.

A few days later he woke up in the night with an excruciating pain surging through his body. He twisted in the bed, listening to the strange grunts he made when the pulsating pain grew too much to bear, especially in the region of his heart. He seemed to hear the sound of tiny teeth methodically working their way through his edible mass.

Like a succulent plant being stripped of its leaves and flowers.

His thoughts turned to Ariel in her scruffy bungalow, all by herself and struggling with her delusions. Should he not have stayed and helped her?

This pain is psychosomatic, he told himself.

But before long he began to wonder; her predictions came back to him. The pain turned to waves of cramp passing across his skin with a sort of churning effect that he recognized from the evening in the hammock, as if his muscles were being resynchronized by maggots moving in ranks beneath his skin, passing like an infestation of locusts from one organ to another.

His heart—he felt—had already been vanquished, replaced by a tight ring of maggots flexing their tiny bodies to pump the diminishing bloodflow through his disappearing veins. The hours passed in excruciating torment. At first light when he left his bed to go to the bathroom, he was stunned with fear when he filled the toilet bowl half to the rim with thick red blood and unspeakable lumps he dared not even think about.

She was right, he thought, glittering with sharp terror.

He'd read somewhere that when the human body comes to the end of its life, the mind often goes through a moment of light-headed clarity. But if these were his final moments, how could it be that he felt himself trembling with such energy— like a battery fully charged? He felt strong enough to kick the door down and sprint up and down the hills for miles. And how could he explain this sudden raging hunger that drove him into the kitchen, where he methodically worked his way through an entire honey melon and peeled off slice after slice of sticky prosciutto, swallowing almost without chewing?

As he stood there, he felt another spasm of hemorrhaging, as if another major organ had just been consumed. Quickly he reached for the sponge. How much blood was there in a man, he asked himself? At what point did the heart resignedly admit that it was only pumping air?

The blood continued running down his legs, collecting in a pool around his feet. Liters and liters of blood. A rivulet started moving across the kitchen floor towards the cooker. He picked up a mop, and cleaned it up. As he worked, the gush turned to a trickle. Then stopped.

After taking a quick brackish shower beneath the rumbling spout, he pulled on a pair of baggy canvas trousers, laced up his shoes and stood in the kitchen, arrested by the sight of his painting of the cone-shaped mountain. Sunlight, entering through the top half of his kitchen window, was illuminating its high ramparts, where a stratospheric wind seemed to be attempting to clear a few whisks of cloud. He saw the figure of Ariel leaning out to hang a shirt on the washing line. But when he leaned in closer he saw that it was just the top half of a human skin.

What seemed beyond all doubt now was that Ariel had knowingly passed on her parasite. Which meant that everything else she'd said was also true. Including her invitation for him to go with them to Switzerland.

He closed the door behind him but left it unlocked and stood on the front step for a moment, listening to the swifts. It was a familiar sound, reminding him of long empty afternoons.

I am not like you, he thought, watching their darting forms. You always come back. But I won't.

7.

Alain was pretty decent about it. Michael turned up in the middle of the morning news bulletin, but he was invited in and given a syrupy coffee from a blackened pot, topped up with milk that had boiled and formed mucous membranes.

Ceremoniously, Alain turned off the television and sat down with a grave frown.

"Are you troubled, my dear boy? You look troubled."

Michael thought about it, and oddly enough decided that he wasn't.

"Actually I just came to say goodbye."

"Off to England, are you?"

"No. To Switzerland."

There was a ponderous pause, while Alain turned the bread he was frying in deep oil, cracking a few eggs also and tipping them in. Alain didn't have much of a notion of healthy eating. He filled two plates and put one of them in front of Michael, nodding at him with a simple, monkish exhortation: "Eat, my son."

Michael obliged, whilst launching into an explanation. "There's been a bit of a development. I met a girl."

"Aha." Alain's eyes flashed like a checkered flag. "And she's broken your heart?"

"No…"

"Taken your tranquility? Involved you in bestial practices?"

"Alain, it's nothing you could ever understand."

"Ah, well, that's true, I've spent my life avoiding the tainting influence of women. It's a question of control, Michael. The minute one lets them in close they start to colonize one. Women have fearsome appetite for territory. They start to till the ground and prepare for the next generation. They're dynastic and not quite in command of their own desires, poor things." He stopped with a shrewd glint in his eye. "I saw her, of course, that peripatetic thing. A handsome girl, very likely devilish, I'd say."

"Certainly devilish, yes. I sort of liked her."

"Of course you did, you liked her for all the wrong reasons."

"I was wondering if you might be able to call your friend, the retired doctor."

"Ah! I might have known…"

"It's not what you think."

"Indeed…" Alain went to his telephone. Michael listened to his homely voice echoing comfortably between the seasoned walls.

Ten minutes later the doctor's knotty hand tapped the window before he pushed the door open and stepped inside, greeting Alain with a meaningful glance and casting his eyes on Michael as if he were an ailing bull in the farmyard. "So here he is," he murmured through his nicotine-stained moustache. "Nothing that a jab won't set straight. Not to worry, young man. What are your symptoms?"

"It started this morning, on the toilet," said Michael, but he thought it best not to tell him how much blood he'd lost.

"Of course it did…" said Alain.

"I'm bleeding."

"Yes, you are, bleeding for your sins, I'd say," said the doctor, holding his stethoscope against Michael's chest; then gave it a puzzled shake. "Strange. I've had this thing since 1953, it's made in France, you know. But now it's packed up. Not to worry, though, I don't expect you're having a cardiac arrest."

When he took Michael's blood pressure, his eyebrows shot up and stayed there like a pair of rampant caterpillars. He pumped up his equipment a few more times and tried again, as if to assure himself that he wasn't mistaken, then asked Alain to come and have a word with him in private.

The two men talked in low voices behind a frosted glass door.

When they came back they looked conspiratorial and ill at ease.

"Am I dying?"

"Not yet, you're not," said the doctor, then corrected himself. "We don't know what's wrong with you, all we know is your blood pressure's zero…"

"And when that happens I have to call a church official in Toulouse… it's regulations," Alain filled in. "They know about this problem you're having; they can help you."

"A church official? What's the church got to do with this?"

The doctor's old face softened, as if speaking to a child. "You don't have a wife, Michael. Have you been seeing *putaines*? Technically speaking there's nothing wrong with it, as long as proper precautions are taken."

"I haven't seen any *putaines*," said Michael defensively.

"And the girl… the one who's been walking about in the village?"

"I only had an ice cream with her."

"I'm very sorry." Alain mopped his forehead and looked, more than anything, thoroughly frightened.

Michael noticed that they both kept themselves on the other side of the kitchen table, as if they were afraid he might at any minute attack them. Though he tried to be unobtrusive about it, the doctor busied himself putting things back in his doctor's case and did not stop until he had surreptitiously laid his hand on a scalpel.

Twenty minutes later two security men came to take him away. One was tall and thin in a tight-fitting brown suit, a classic pedophile type with a receding chin, simpering eyes and trousers finishing halfway up his ankles. The other was short and squat, in a cream-colored suit, his face hidden behind steel-rim aviator sunglasses, like a cocaine dealer from *Grand Theft Auto*.

"Where are we going?" Michael asked as he was led away. Oddly enough he was not afraid of them, though he felt he probably should be.

The short one turned round and gave him a look of unmistakable brutality. "You go where we go, kiddo. And we go wherever we want. Now zip it! We're not here to listen to the likes of you."

They'd parked a black vintage Citroën outside. A few kids were standing there admiring it as Michael emerged with the men, who'd handcuffed him.

After an hour's drive they rolled up outside a secure psychiatric unit with guards at the gates. The car door opened; he was dragged out and jostled into a gray corridor with a highly polished floor squeaking under his sneakers.

"Where are you taking me? What's the matter with you?" he cried at the nurses, but to his surprise one of them got out a rubber baton and walloped him a few times. Unceremoniously he was dumped in a small, blank cell. He lay on the floor as he listened to the fading squeaks of their gym shoes.

Humanoid waste, piece of shit, deserves to die and will...

After he'd calmed himself down, he sat up against the door, staring at his shoelaces for an hour. Occasionally the waves of pain inside returned, but all in all he was clearer than he'd been in years; in fact, although he was in a cell, he felt he'd started on his road to Damascus. Thank God.

He thought of Ariel, how he had to find her, had to get back to her. Everything she said had turned out to be true. What slaves we are, he said to himself. What slaves to convention. Our lives are lies.

Night fell and as he lay on his bunk he seemed to hear thousands of tiny voices inside his body, all reciting together as they worked tirelessly to ensure their survival.

There was something intrinsically gentle about maggots: the way they rubbed softly against their neighbors without chafing. Their black, tiny eyes, devoid of expression or feeling. A multitude of maggots was almost like a body of water, modest in all its demands, always finding the lowest, simplest, and most direct path.

He imagined Ariel in front him. "Through meeting you I have become like you," he whispered into the darkness. "For good or ill you have transformed me."

But he knew he was in trouble, because he was prettifying the words.

8.

In spite of his predicament, the mere idea of being with Ariel again as an equal filled Michael with energy. Now that they were both maggot people, would it be different when they were together? Would he also become telepathic?

As night set in and the hospital lay steeped in thunderous silence, he seemed to hear Ariel's voice quite clearly in his head.

"Michael, there'll be time later to think about love and telepathy and a lot of other overrated things. But now you have to escape. There's an incinerator in the hospital grounds. Tomorrow they'll take you there and burn you. It's the only sure way of killing the maggots without any of them getting away."

"They must really hate the maggots."

"Yes, they say they're a threat to democracy and civilization. But when you think about it, in a maggot world there'd be no war, there'd be no inequality or cruelty. Maggots ask for very little, just food and oxygen... that's the bargain between the maggot and the human. Do you understand?"

Her voice faded.

He looked up and found himself staring at the padded corners of the cell, the heavy-duty polyurethane window frames, reinforced panes and a small air vent in the wall. With some difficulty he broke the grille with his shoe and elbow, then reached into the cavity, removed the plastic grille on the other side, and, for no particular reason he could think of, pushed out his shoes and clothes.

For an hour or more he sat naked and cross-legged on the floor like a long-suffering Buddha, unsure of what to do next.

Until he felt a tickling sensation along his arm.

He looked down. His skin was literally splitting down the inside of his wrist. White maggots in their thousands were spilling out. He watched his body deflating until he lay like a hand-puppet on the floor. Soon the "bone maggots" were collapsing his cranium. Everything grew silent and dark.

Had he been able to see himself, it would have been a strange sight: his most delicate parts such as his inner ears were being picked up like weird flesh trumpets and furtively passed along ranks of squirming maggots. Michael was only conscious of a gray world, like a flickering television screen without a signal, no physical sensation at all, no awareness of what was happening. But there was consciousness.

Meanwhile, his entire body was on the march. Millions of maggots pulled his empty skin along—like an army of ants tugging at a butterfly—then carefully maneuvered it through the dusty, jagged hole. Getting the brain through was tricky, particularly as the eyeballs were still attached to their optical nerves. The maggots took infinite care not to damage the delicate tissue. Occasionally they reassembled around the brain, feeding it oxygen and preventing it from dehydrating. And on the other side they gently pullulated around it as they slowly slid down a drainpipe into the grass.

A few hours before dawn, Michael began to take shape again and his vision and hearing returned. Also his physical sense of self—his use of arms and legs. He stood up and dusted himself down, relieved to be back in charge of his faculties and somewhat surprised to find himself in the garden outside the hospital. It seemed to him now (and ever afterwards) that the physical world was a sort of illusion facilitated by his body, a construct of his physical senses.

He climbed the perimeter fence and walked into a tinder-dry forest. His mind was distracted. A part of him was still in that parallel universe he'd temporarily entered.

He walked through the world as if he were experiencing it for the first time. Moonlight had magically transformed the olive groves into billowing seas of silver. Crickets were grinding deafeningly—a host of sewing machines secreted in the trees. The air teemed with insects. Overhead, he heard and saw a bat crunch its microscopic teeth into a moth. From an adjacent field beyond a stone wall came the slightly absurd and almost mythical braying of an ass, exactly like a creaking water-pump. There was a sacred language to all this, a language humans no longer understood.

He followed a dry watercourse to the bottom of the hill, where he rejoined the road and waited for Ariel, whose arrival seemed imminent. He had a sense of her setting off at this very moment from the decrepit bungalow by the sea where the rollers were still breaking with repeating thunder. He saw her pale face through the windscreen. He saw Günter's lolloping gait as he leapt into the back through the sliding door. Probably the engine started on the third try, after some cursing. And their wheels spun in the deep sand as they climbed the rutted track, leaving wheel marks that the wind would quickly rub out after they had gone.

9.

After they had picked him up, they travelled for hour after hour down the motorway, with the parched hills stretching out on either side. Everything was dry, everything was dreaming of water, but water there was none.

Ariel was more at ease than he had seen her before, no longer nerve-racked. She concentrated on her driving and seemed to have a notion of being on their way and nominally at least going *somewhere*.

Michael felt strange in their company, like a refugee among an unknown people. All the emotional intensity he had first felt about Ariel seemed utterly ludicrous now. Hindsight is a terrible companion, filled with the "could-have-done" or "should-be." Sitting in the van, looking out glumly at the passing hills, he felt he was being overrun by conditionals.

Günter was lying on an old rug in the back, peering intently into a copy of Houellebecq's *Platform* and awkwardly turning and creasing the pages with his humid nose. From time to time their eyes met in the mirror. Finally, stung by Michael's glances, the Alsatian looked up and said to him: "In case you're wondering… my name is Günter. I'm a person; I was even born somewhere, admittedly somewhere not very spectacular. I consider myself an Austrian but I don't expect the Austrians would agree."

"I never said you weren't a person."

"Sometimes people don't need to say very much; you can tell what they're thinking."

"Well I wish I knew what to think and I wish I knew where we were going."

"Oh, I shouldn't worry about that," said Günter with a glimmer of a smile and a nod at Ariel: "She may be keeping very quiet but she's feeling very decisive. Those long weeks in that god-awful cabin with nothing but the sun and that brutal sea. It grilled the truth out of her; she's begun to understand there's no choice but to come in. Right, Ariel?"

"Come in where?" said Michael.

Ariel turned her head and looked at him. "We're going to a place where maggot people go for collection… to be processed, basically."

Again, Michael felt the churning of hindsight in his stomach, the fierceness of his regret. "You make it sound like a meatpacking plant."

Ariel was humorless about it. "When people die, Michael, what happens to them? Shall I tell you? They're cleaned and prepared and wrapped in winding-sheets, then they're laid out in a box and either buried or incinerated."

"So what?"

"And we're no different. The only difference is we don't take it so seriously."

There was a silence while Michael tried to work up the courage to say the obvious thing. He was reluctant to do so in case it led to derision. "Why do you keep talking about being dead, Ariel? You're not dead. Why don't you think about something more cheerful?"

Günter cracked up in the back. "You hear that, girl? Think about something more cheerful."

Ariel didn't bother replying to that one. She kept her hands steadily on the wheel and seemed to enjoy pushing the old van to its maximum speed as they clattered down the motorway, occasionally managing to squeeze past a smoky old lorry.

After those few moments of peace and quiet, Ariel punched the steering wheel and broke into long-winded cursing. "Would you believe it?" she cried, shaking her head at Günter. "They're starting."

"Starting what?" said Michael, finding that Ariel was staring at him with a vaguely infuriated expression on her face.

"You waited too long, that's why," said Günter. "You waited for Mr. Ferdinand here and now the countdown's started."

"I can feel it. They're starting. What I mean is I *can't* feel it. I can't feel my feet, I can't feel my legs! They're sleeping; they're dying."

"Is that my fault?" Michael threw in.

For the first time there was something raw about her face, meaning that her emotions were simmering to the surface like volcanic bubbles as she turned to him and with an almost amused expression on her face, as if she were entering the world of absurdity, asked in a very matter-of-fact voice: "Where will you go without me?"

"Why would I go anywhere without you?"

"Poor you, you don't know anything," said Ariel. "About your situation. There's a whole maggot world out there you know nothing about. Meeting me was bad luck for you. I told you from the start… I won't do as I'm told; that's my problem. I don't want to be one of *them*."

"Who, for God's sake?"

She winced again with the effort of explaining. "The maggot survivors, I call them. A bunch of fuck-ups who spend their time in purple robes, prolonging their meaningless lives and inventing a lot of useless shit."

She grew silent, and Michael decided not to probe her, even though he was thoroughly mystified. Purple robes? Who wore purple robes? Priests? He opened his mouth to speak, but when he looked at Ariel he stopped himself. Her blanched face was wrinkled up like a concertina. She let go of the steering wheel and clutched her forehead with a moan: "They're eating me, the little bastards."

From the back of the van he heard Günter's voice: "Michael, if I were you, I'd grab that wheel."

He took the Alsatian's advice. Stunned, Ariel slid to the floor with her fingertips pressed to her temples. He clambered over into the driver's seat while she dragged herself into the back. The kilometers slid by like slow contractions.

The petrol gauge was almost on zero.

Ariel spoke from the floor: "Take the next exit; get off the motorway."

No sooner had she spoken than he saw a sign, then a slip-road running down a long incline bordered by tall yellow mustard flowers and wild poppies.

"Turn right at the top. Follow the signs to Vegnier-du-Lac."

Again, he followed her instructions. They drove for another twenty minutes.

She remained on the floor, concentrating on the grisly thing taking place inside her head: tiny, mulching maggot mouths pressing against her cerebral cortex, gobbling at her nerve endings, muzzling their tiny lips against her emotions.

The warning light was flashing on the fuel gauge. They had no money left—they'd spent the last of it that morning on a cheese baguette.

Michael wondered how he would break it to Ariel that very soon they'd be marooned in the middle of a flat, barren landscape bisected by a long straight road studded on both sides with rows of white-painted poplars.

"Almost there," said Ariel. "When you see a large field on the left full of deep blue lavender, hang a left. The road runs straight through it." She winced and continued, although she was racked with pain: "There it is; take the next left, a gravel track with a string of grass and boulders in the middle. Just keep going…"

Michael saw the track and turned off. They drove through a fragrant landscape, banks of lavender on either side. Ariel wound her window down and breathed deep.

"Good. See the white house, that's where we're going."

Up ahead he saw a cottage embedded within flowering shrubs, fruit trees, and a mountainous rose espalier, the scent of which hit him with a druglike heaviness. Ariel groaned. "Stop by the gate, I can't walk… and then go knock on the door. Be quick, please."

Michael's eyes narrowed as he saw a slight figure, a woman in a long flowing dress standing by the wicker gate. She was holding a double-barreled shotgun that seemed almost longer and heavier than she was.

"She's got a gun."

"It's only Purissima," Günter commented in the back. "She's a terrible shot."

Along the last few bumpy yards of the boulder-strewn track, the engine choked with a last-ditch lurch. The woman tapped the barrel of her rifle against the glass.

"Get out, Günter. I'm not putting this thing down until I've searched the car." She nodded towards Michael. "Who's that man with you?"

"Don't worry about him," said Günter. "He's harmless."

10.

Only when Purissima drew closer did Michael see how tiny she was: jet black hair and a birdlike body made of sticks and wire and peppercorn eyes that knew everything in an instant. She reached barely to his chest. When she spoke she had an unsettling habit of moving in closer and closer, opening her mouth as she did so, like a spacecraft docking. The listener usually found himself retreating: there is something unpleasant about an open mouth. Lips are nature's clever disguise, a decorative rim to the digestive tract.

Günter jumped out of the van and shook himself, apologetic and somewhat ill-at-ease. "Hello, Purissima. We're back."

"Of course you're back; you were always coming back. Ariel looks ready for the cemetery, I can practically smell the corpse already." Her voice smattered like shiny rivets flung angrily at a tiled floor: rapid-firing pidgin English with strong Spanish, possibly Mexican, roots.

Günter yawned. "Maybe. She has pain... and numbness."

"Pain and numbness... pain and numbness..." Purissima shook her head, filled with a pleasurable regret. "Those twins I've lived with for so long I don't even notice them no more. They don't kill you, that's the only good thing to be said of them." Purissima spun round and led them down the garden path, after throwing Michael a skew-whiff gaze and murmuring into his ear: "You're her latest lamb, I suppose?" Before Michael could respond, Purissima clapped her hands: "Quick, quick. Bring her round. I will make a bed for her, I will fetch herbs."

She disappeared with a swish of her skirts.

"Fucking herbs!" said Günter. "Mumbo jumbo. It's medievalism, it's the jester's fucking cap and bells round the ankle… know what I mean?" His hairy loins and swinging scrotum trotted off as he sought out some shade at the bottom of the garden under overhanging trees.

Ariel climbed out of the Transit with infinite care, as if she had a razor blade lodged in her innards. "Give me your hand."

They stumbled round the white wooden house, along burgeoning flowerbeds. At the back, a tourist bed had already been placed in the middle of a large rose garden. Purissima returned with a basket of ointments and immediately began helping Ariel out of her sweat-soaked clothes, rubbing rose oil into her scalp and neck. Michael stood indecisively at her side, wanting to help but not quite knowing what to do. He sat down in the grass, watching, not speaking. An hour passed, then Purissima took his arm and whispered, more slowly now:

"Come inside with me. She must sleep." As they made their way back to the house, she continued: "They've retreated slightly. Confused. Rose oil has a restorative effect on the system. The massage has to be repeated every four hours. But you have to stay away from her. Do not touch her, do you understand? Keep your filthiness away from my precious love."

"Will she die?"

"One day we all die; even *you*. We leave our precious skins on the floor, we step out of the cage and we're free."

"When… will she die?" he persevered.

"Oh, when her time comes." She raised her sharp little fist and shook it in front of Michael's chin, then stalked off with a muttered curse.

Later, Michael tracked down Günter, who was sitting with his back to them, looking out over the lavender fields. "Sorry if I don't turn round," said Günter. "The wind is right in my face. I'm in lavender heaven."

"No, no… I only came to ask…"

"You want to know what's happening. Okay. It's really not much more than a grand tragedienne mystifying what any fool could see. Drop a lump of shit from a very great height and watch what happens next."

"Who are you Günter? I'd like to know."

"I can tell you but it will take a little time."

"Could you annotate?"

"I like you when you're sarcastic, Michael; it's so much better than your shocked-little-boy act. You should really cultivate sarcasm." His black dog-lips parted in what one might choose to see as a smile. "Very well, for you I will annotate," he said.

11.

"I was a weak-spirited young man," said Günter. "In myself I had nothing, I was born with a love of my mother's breast and I did not move beyond this love of the breast. I grew up in East Germany. In those days it was a brutal place; there was every opportunity for weak persons to be decorated with medals and insignia as a way of labeling themselves, quickly and conveniently explaining their status and identity. Even when I was a boy, they put me in a uniform and taught me to shoot and march. A private has to salute more or less any scum in uniform, signifying that he respects the other person's rank and defers to him. This is about as low as human life can get, Michael. We were all very keen on it in those days, everyone had to have a label on him, thank Christ they hadn't invented bar codes yet… we would have spent our whole fucking lives going through scanners."

"What period are you in?"

"After the war," said Günter. "I am talking about myself and I am annotating."

"You must be old, then?"

"Old. Yes, I am old. You can't see my age in my face, but you wouldn't have recognized me back then, either. I was very fond of marching about and saluting as soon as I saw some shit coming along with polished boots and vodka on his breath and his red nose stuck up in the air. People were big on sticking their noses in the air; they felt they were very important and had to tell everyone about it." His eyes blinked intently. "You know, I think it's the main reason why Marx came up with his socialist claptrap. The workers in their lumpy old clogs must have got pissed off in the end when the haughty ones came marching past in their shiny boots, waving their brand new guns. Jealousy, I think it's the only human emotion."

"You were going to tell me who you were, Günter."

"One needs a bit of detail to do it properly. I could tell you about a section of wall I had to guard. People always think all the guards were posted around the fucking Brandenburg Gate, but most of us were stuck in some god-awful village full of stinking peasants. We lived on sauerkraut and sausage; we felt it was good enough for us, as long as it was meat we felt we were doing all right. The only good part was I had a decent girlfriend. She was a cook in a hospital canteen; she used to iron my clothes and make porridge in the evenings. I don't know where she was from, she must have been Armenian or something, she squelched like mud in the bedroom but I couldn't get her pregnant however hard I tried. Later I realised she was a maggot girl. Little bitch filled me with them too; then she died. I went over the fence after that, claimed political asylum and hitchhiked down to Rome. It didn't take me long to hang up my uniform and join a religious order. I was a novice for a few years. The rest is history."

"You know Günter, I'm starting to suspect you of being a bit of a liar."

"Oh, I am. Lying is what one has to do if one wants to convince people of anything. Even history is a lie; it's a massive constructed lie. Religion is the hugest lie of them all."

"No wonder they turned you into a dog. I would have turned you into a something strange, like an anteater."

"The only truth," said Günter, "is that air comes in and out of your nostrils."

Across the garden Ariel was once again being massaged by Purissima.

"Is her time up?" said Michael.

"Oh, she has time enough. Time we have. Life we don't have," said Günter. "Speed is not something I admire anyway. Speed is a rejection of everything I like; a love of speed may even be a disease of sorts. I'd like to dissect the brains of people who like motorbikes. For the good of the human race. I mean turn them into medical research."

"Is this your idea of annotation?"

Günter looked at him with narrowing eyes. "There is something about you that surprises me, Michael. You seem quite small, but once you open your mouth, one begins to sense there's more substance."

"I thought we were talking about you?"

"Yes. We were. I was a kid as well, a long time ago. After the war, after all the shits in uniforms were rounded up by the Americans and the Russians and either shot or packed into trains and taken away, I went into the hills and threw away my uniform and learned about cows and milking and making cheese. They were good years. I rarely went to the bottom of the valley; I stayed around the high pastures and hardly spoke to anyone except the farmer I was working for. It was at this time that I first got interested in religion. I suppose the paraphernalia interested me, the cloaks and vestments and candles and rituals and crossing oneself at every opportunity; it was more or less the same as the army, except in the spiritual world all the killing would be done by a higher power." He raised his paw, to make a distinction: "And interestingly one would not be killed until after one had already died. I am speaking of damnation, of course. God would fling one into a burning pit if one had not done one's duty. I liked this, it freed humans from the awful necessity of butchering each other; at least that's what I thought at the time. I went for it hook, line and sinker. But before I could act on it I was arrested. They put a gun in my hand and told me to start patrolling and shoot anyone I saw. It seemed reasonable for a while."

"Maybe you should write a book about your life, Günter."

"I can see you are laughing at me, Michael. In fact I did write a book. It didn't do very well. I think it was banned, either by the Russians or the East Germans. My theories were no crazier than theirs, but humans always get murderous if anyone comes up with a different theory, especially if it involves any sort of religious ideas. God help the man who expresses any kind of opinion about the color of God's beard. Wake up, fuckers, God does not have a beard and beards do not have a God to attach themselves to; they float around aimlessly in space. Most wars have been fought over details, Michael. What sort of trousers you should wear? Should you eat cow hocks or boiled fish? Is it correct to play a mandolin? Should you wear your hair long or shave your head?" He growled. "It makes my teeth itch; it makes me want to sink them into a larded, pompous ass."

"And then?"

"Well, after I took holy orders in Rome I had even more problems, most of them because I wouldn't respect some shit because of his cloak. You know my name should not be Günter at all. It should be 'Will You Excuse Me If I'm Fucking Unimpressed?' Because that's been the theme of my life. Always." He lay down his head. "And now I don't care anymore. I've seen the progression of the human race, I remember those beautiful mountains when I was a young man. A few years after the war, a lot of shits with skis started showing up in the winters. The landowner cut long swaths through the trees and put up ski lifts. More and more shits started coming for the skiing, crowding the bars, eating cheese fondue and drinking copious amounts of beer. The amount of fucking going on was mind-boggling; they were worse than hogs. Maggots were hatching like locusts, spilling out everywhere." He rolled onto his back and sighed pleasurably. "I wish people could try and appreciate how lovely it is to lie still and smell the grass."

"I guess they want to be a bit more dynamic."

"You know," said Günter, "I knew a guy once; he was a filthy guy covered in tattoos and he lived in a cave and he only had two brown teeth left in his mouth. Do you want to know what he did for a living? He made soap, that's what. And he scented it with flowers."

"I don't get the connection."

"That's what we are, that's who I am… and you too. We're the filthy ones who make soap, but we never wash ourselves…"

12.

In the morning when Michael woke up he vaguely remembered having been massaged in the night with essential oils, rose and something like lavender and sandalwood.

"For protection," whispered Ariel with a smile, adding, "We are safe here. Purissima knows how to handle them."

Michael looked at her. "What happened to you yesterday?"

"It's all so unnatural," said Ariel.

"What is?"

"When they want more *lebensraum* you really don't have much of a choice. They start to multiply; you feel them pressing against the inside of your skin, and you know you have to start looking for the pressure valve."

"The pressure valve?"

"Sex…" She laughed, tears glittering in her eyes. "We don't own our bodies anymore. We can't do what we want with them. The only time they ever let me feel sexual excitement is when I'm with a straight man. I mean a man who's not been maggotized."

"So the first time we slept together…"

"…was incredible. I must have had twenty-five orgasms that night. Maggot orgasms, you know—simulated orgasms because your body no longer has the ability to… I mean, they just send the impulses up to the brain. I even had an orgasm when I came out to speak with you the first time. That's why all I could think of to say was that silly thing about ice cream. Who cares about stupid orgasms, anyway? I'm tired of them, personally."

"So it's just procreation for them?"

Ariel laughed. "Yes. For them. Go forth and multiply. That old chestnut. They reward sexually aggressive behavior with strangers. That way they find new host bodies." Her face clouded over. "But they take away a woman's ability to have a child. They rob her of that. Not maliciously. They don't think; they don't do it on purpose. But all the most evil things are senseless mechanisms. A snake, the way it lashes out and bites you without even thinking about it. A tsunami. Are these things evil? I would say they are. Probably even maggots are evil."

Michael sat up in shock, the realization striking home. "So when you told me that thing about how good the maggots were it was just bullshit!"

"*Ach*," she said, "you were ripe for the taking. Anyway, you had a tumor, you were seriously ill." She met his accusing stare. "Michael, if I apologized to you now it would be an empty gesture. I knew what I was doing when I picked you up. I'd probably do it again if I had to. I found myself a Provençal backwater, a village full of repressed, sad fuckers with generations of stupefied lunatics behind them. Moldering scar tissue in their attics. I put on my best dress and I walked fresh as a daisy through the village square until some dolt of a peasant came sniffing at me. By that I mean *you*, of course. I have to admit you were more sophisticated than most peasants I've had. Men who pick you flowers in a ditch and come to you with dried sweat in their armpits. With callused, dirty hands… smelling of shit, red wine, and cheap aftershave. They ask you to marry them as soon as you wake up after the first night of fucking… because they want a woman to do the cooking and cleaning, someone they can screw when they come home in the evening."

He breathed hard, trying to contain his panic. "How did it first happen? I mean the maggots."

"It was this *mierda*. A German immigrant from the south of Brazil. Tall blond creep. He delivered the gas bottles to my parents' hotel. My mother used to talk to him, give him coffee in the kitchen. She liked him, or lusted after him, more like. He had very thick arms covered in hair and his face was always very brown and shiny like mahogany. His chest looked like a tree trunk, his legs like two thinner tree trunks bolted together at the top. And his crotch bulged like a mozzarella cheese hung up to dry. My father was always at work... he was a very good worker ant. Convenient for my mother."

"Ariel, is there anything you respect?"

"Yes. People who shut up." She laughed. "You know, Michael, I actually *like* you, and that's bloody rare. Anyway, I think my mother used to suck him off in the kitchen sometimes."

"How can you talk about your mother like that?"

"Oh God, you really are a peasant; you even respect mothers. They're just women who got knocked up."

"Where do you come into it?"

"I told you. Maggot folk need to fuck real people, or they die. They try to keep it low key, sort of like normal humans going to the toilet." She trembled with revulsion. "Anyway, back to Ricardo. One day he just walked into my bedroom with his tree-trunk legs. I was eighteen years old. His testicles were so full of maggots they looked like drum skins." She laughed uneasily, but her eyes clouded over. "It was kind of a fantasy of mine that he would come into my room, see me on the bed... and then nature would take its course. Except I hadn't thought about what it would really be like having an ugly shit like that pumping away at my ovaries. So you see," she sighed resignedly, "my whole family was transformed into maggot folk, all in the aid of Ricardo getting his rocks off. Eventually their doctor sent them off to a hospital... where they were incinerated... for the benefit of the human race."

"Christ, it's barbaric," said Michael.

"The only good part," she said, "is that maggots get old, too. They quieten down, eat their beans, and shut up."

She was interrupted by the sound of a creaking door.

Purissima came barefooted across the grass, a secretive smile on her face as if pleased to have these two visitants lying like pods between her flowering roses. She dipped her hands in rose oil. "Off with your nightshirts," she chimed. "Time for massage, then aloe berries."

"I hate aloe berries," said Ariel.

"So do maggots; aloe makes them less randy and rather docile," said Purissima. "Remember, you are *passengers*…"

13.

Venus passed overhead and faded with morning. When Michael woke, Ariel had also faded. He spent the morning digging a trench for her in a walled cemetery at the bottom of the garden, whilst Purissima's wailing from the house occasionally wafted down to him. He listened to the sound his spade made, and the soil piling up. By the time he'd finished, Purissima had anointed the body and placed it in a small casket.

When he saw Michael's devastation, Günter licked his nostrils clean and said, "You know you mustn't take cessation of life so seriously. It's only emotion, and emotion passes. Plus, when you think about it, nothing actually exists anyway. Everything… absolutely everything… is just one big illusion. A crock of shit, you might say."

"Only a moment ago she was right here. Now she's gone."

"She was never here in the first place," said Günter. "And neither are you."

When Michael stroked her cheek, he sensed an enormously distant response: a faint rustling of wind through the leaves of a forest. But he knew that Ariel was now in that world he had experienced once, the gray flickering world of the dead television screen.

"Let her go," said Günter. "She's happier there than she ever was here."

Before they lowered her into the earth, Purissima screwed an air intake into a purpose-made duct in the coffin. They scooped back the soil and stood there looking at the grave. The small metal chimney was equipped with a tiny fan, turning in the wind. He let his eyes sweep across the little cemetery, and he realized there was a slightly discordant feeling about the graves around him: they all had the same metal pipes poking out of the ground, and the same glittering, spinning air intakes.

Günter cleared his throat. "Where will you go now?"

"Does it matter?"

"Some would say it does matter. You must go to Cannes, you must find a woman called Janine. Can you memorize an address?" He gave him a house number and a street name.

After Purissima had gone, Michael sat there pushing his hand into the dry, warm loam and wondering how Ariel felt, lying down there in the darkness. As he dug his hand deeper he felt the moisture; he saw insects crawling; worms, centipedes and even hundreds of squirming maggots working their way up towards light. They had abandoned Ariel like rats. Crawling things, blind things, mindless scrabbling, churning things.

At the close of that first endless day, Michael felt long languid convolutions running through his body, and it sank home that his spirit was now entirely in conflict with his physical self. He felt a slithering under his skin, listened to the moist rustling of their tiny, waxed bodies, those dumb black heads and jaws chewing endless wormholes through everything that stood in their way.

He hated his limbs, his torso. He thought: "God rot this fucking bag of shit."

That evening he sat in the rose garden until the sun went down, then waited for the moon to rise. Mosquitoes swarmed around him, attracted by his heat but confused by his bloodless body.

Early in the morning he tapped on Purissima's door to ask for money; then tramped off with a petrol can down the long lane with its two chalky ruts and grass string in the middle. He returned an hour later with ten liters of fuel, which he emptied into the tank of the old Transit and fired her up.

Günter was nowhere to be seen. There were no farewells. Purissima's white knuckles parted a curtain in a window and her tremulous face hovered there momentarily. Already spent, like a memory.

14.

By the time Michael got to Cannes, there was a cool evening breeze, and people were sitting in bars, enjoying liquid refreshments. He sat in the fading light, watching a parade of humanity: men like puffed-up balloons of self-importance clutching colorful women with painted, surgically manipulated faces.

Loneliness blew like a cool wind round his heart. The feeling of agitation grew until he wanted to beat his fists against the table and cry out for help.

Who in this world cared about him?

He went into a grocery shop and bought himself a cheap bottle of vodka. The alcohol seemed to deaden his system without affecting his clarity of mind. The slight dulling effect was just what he was looking for. He bought another bottle and drained that, too, standing in the street.

Twenty meters down the road just as he turned the corner, he was hit by a wave of alcohol that almost knocked him off his feet. As he crawled into an empty alley, he understood that the maggots must finally have absorbed more than they could take. His hosts were evidently trying to decipher this strange energy running through their primitive systems. His skin churned, throwing up crests and ripples. He lay back, blind drunk, no longer caring what happened to him. Next to his head a bag of refuse had disgorged its fish-stinking contents.

But the maggots reasserted control. There was a moment of extreme discomfort, then he felt his skin sweating profusely. A trickle of vodka came pushing out through his pores, until he lay there sober and foolish, smelling like a distillery. Sensation returned to his body: a jagged edge was digging into his hip, his hand was glued to a sticky patch on the ground.

The maggots seemed angry now, and rather turbulent. You've had your fun, they seemed to be saying. Now we want ours.

Michael got up and felt his limbs surging with energy.

Ten minutes later he was sitting on a lumpy bed in a cheap hostel, staring at a tin ashtray and plywood cupboard whose doors kept yawning open every few minutes until he wedged them with a folded bit of paper. Sleep did not seem possible. The walls reeked of mold; the cracked sink in a corner stank of urine. But the shower cubicle beckoned and, although there was a slimy feeling about the rubber mat, he threw down his dirty clothes and trod soap suds into them under the tepid drizzle.

The night was pleasantly cool. He kept the window wide open and hung his clothes from the curtain rail, letting the breeze waft them dry. Lying on the bed with the lights off, he smoked one cigarette after another. There was no need to worry about his lungs anymore. The maggots expanded and contracted inside him to simulate breathing. As they drew the smoke in, they worked to rid themselves of the nicotine.

Poisons seemed to keep the maggot busy. Maybe a maggot person even needed copious amounts of alcohol, drugs, and nicotine to stay healthy? It also occurred to him that if one absorbed too much poison, the maggots might falter and die off? Surely they were normal organisms susceptible to disease?

For a while he thought about Ariel and how he missed her. He remembered how once she had told him that every time one lost something, one gained something else in its place, which one wouldn't otherwise have found.

He wondered what he could possibly gain by the loss of Ariel.

It seemed an inconceivable question.

That first morning in Cannes wasn't really a morning at all, just a sort of half-lit dawn beneath a sky of ragged-tail clouds, hounded by the mistral. His trousers had blown out of the window in the night, ending up in the narrow cul-de-sac below. For a moment he lay there wondering why he had woken so early. Then realized *they* must have roused him for some reason. Quickly he pulled on his damp boxer shorts and T-shirt, then carefully opened the door and listened to the murmur of voices from the reception desk.

Tiptoeing over the corridor's dirty tiles, he peered into the reception at two lanky, straw-haired Germans with backpacks and walking boots. They looked harmless enough, but they were showing their police badges and telling the proprietor to check the register for recent arrivals.

Back in his room, he scrabbled together his few belongings and went to the window. It was the third floor: a jump would certainly be fatal to any normal person.

The only important thing was to protect his brain; he must hit the ground feet-first, so that the full length of his body acted as a shock absorber.

It was a curious feeling, casually taking a step into the empty air, as if going for a leisurely walk.

He hit the ground with enormous force and, as if in slow-motion, watched his body compress itself into the ground. For a while he lay disfigured and broken on the cobbles. His left leg had snapped clean off against the side of a bin, and the maggots lay in piles all round it, frantically tugging at flaps of skin.

Grabbing his severed leg, he crawled out of sight, hiding himself in a pile of refuse sacks.

In the window overhead he saw the backpackers rifling through his room, then peering down over the windowsill. One of them waved a pistol about.

He waited nervously for the maggots to do their work; pressing the stub of shinbone and foot against what remained of his leg, while the maggots reconnected the two. Waves of pain shot through him; punitive pain of such an excruciating kind that he began to tremble and moan.

Don't jump out of windows, they seemed to be saying. *Don't complicate our lives.*

When he was strong enough to stand, he glanced up at the window to make sure the men weren't there, then gingerly made his way over to where he had hit the ground; the spot was marked by a scattering of maggots in the gutter. He scooped them up, grabbed his trousers and ran for his life.

Twenty minutes later he was in a backstreet bar, studying the maggots in his palm.

"For once you're in my power," he thought. Their white serrated bodies squirmed; their black eyes were no more than specks. "You *look* harmless enough."

He took one of them and cut it in two between the nails of his thumb and index finger. As he did so, he felt a sharp cattle-prod pain at the back of his head. His arms shot out. His glass hit the floor, a chair was knocked over. He recomposed himself, waited a while; then, as an afterthought, put the remaining maggots in his mouth and made himself swallow them. An enormous wave of well-being ran through him; he felt himself ejaculate strongly into his trousers. A phantom ejaculation. *Christ!*

15.

From now on I have to be cleverer, he told himself. I've been driving round in Ariel's rusty van and the registration must be flagged on every police computer in the country. I've been leaving it parked in the street like a fool while I get drunk, and I almost paid for it.

I'm alive. But does my life really matter at all?

What the hell am I doing here?

All day he idled on a disused roof: Cannes lay in disordered profusion all round, palm trees in the squares, café tables invading the pavements, cars parked profusely along the narrow lanes. From the rooftop he also had an excellent view of the Transit, smeared with starling droppings, skulking in the shade of a palm tree. Police technicians had been at the scene since mid-morning, putting up a screen and cordoning off the entire area. They removed all of its contents in black plastic bin liners. A flatbed truck came and picked up the whole damned thing with a pneumatic arm, then drove away.

Later that afternoon, Michael went to find the woman Günter had tipped him off about.

Janine's apartment lay right above a busy restaurant with outside tables in a little flowery square with an ugly, squat war memorial and trickling fountain. As he approached he saw her on the first-floor balcony, basking in the sun like a daubed tropical bird on its nest—wearing an unbuttoned camouflage-pattern boiler suit and a turquoise bikini top encrusted with rhinestones. She peered down at him over the balcony railing, a tall glass of what looked like a Campari soda in her hand. Most of her face was hidden behind a pair of outsized, mirrored sunglasses. "Who are you and what do you want?" she called out before he'd even got close to the doorbell.

He looked up. "I got your details from Günter. He's a four-footed guy from Rome. Excommunicated."

She looked frightened and dropped her voice. "Oh, come on! I don't know you, I don't know him. Just because I live above a restaurant people think they can hit on me."

"I only want to come inside for a few minutes. If I'd come to arrest you I would have brought a friend." He opened his jacket to indicate he was not wearing a holster.

Her shades glittered down at him for a full minute. He waited for her decision. A police siren edged closer. Stepping into the recessed doorway, he pressed himself against the wall. The door buzzed and he quickly pushed it open and moved into the cool gloom, standing there waiting for his imaginary pulse to slow down.

The door squeezed itself shut behind him and he walked up the single flight.

Janine was waiting for him in the doorway, then, without a word, showed him into an apartment almost entirely devoid of furniture. She was clearly a big believer in blowup cushions and paper lanterns. The only thing of substance in there was a leather briefcase, large and fat and black. Everything else was inflatable.

He stepped into the living room, steeped in the sort of silence that follows a hastily evacuated party. Palls of smoke rose erectly from cigarettes left in scattered ashtrays, and six blue Siamese kittens sitting in line fixed him with their blue eyes until one of them made a rash attack on a cushion, which deflated with a hissing sound.

Janine turned to Michael. "This won't take a minute." Then, calling out towards the back of the adjoining room: "Take him!"

Two men charged out, sending the kittens scurrying in all directions. One of them pinned him down, the other used a pair of box-cutters to slice into his stomach. Michael kept his mouth shut, fearing that they might shoot him if he resisted. Peering down, what he saw would have made him retch if he had guts to retch with. His abdomen was open like a bowl of fruit: white warm maggots were squirming, wild to get out of the light.

Janine breathed out. "He's maggot. Close him up."

They folded the skin back and it quickly sealed itself. Janine gave them a nod and they withdrew without a word into the back room. Once they were out of sight there were two metallic clicks—not of guns, but beer cans.

Janine sat down with a sharp squeak on one of her cushions. "Okay, so you're maggot. Doesn't mean very much, I have to say. Anyone could be maggot."

She took off her sunglasses and with a fluid movement removed what proved to be a wig. Beneath, she was clean-shaven with pale eyes like jeans washed too many times. "Sit down." She nodded at a plastic cube and he eased himself into it. "So why are you here? I can't possibly trust you. You could be anyone…"

"I'm not. I was locked up in the hospital but I got out. I did what Ariel said. She got me out. That's all. She didn't believe it either at first. We drove towards Chamonix to see Purissima, but Ariel died." His voice grew tremulous. "I think her poison got to her. She picked a very hard one for herself."

"No one picks their poison," said Janine. "The poison picks you and then we blame it on the maggot. The waste remains and kills you in the end." She stared bleakly at him. "I knew Ariel. I didn't know she'd crossed over, though. And of course Günter with his dirty ass. He used to be a monk, except he was always causing a stink. In the end he pissed off a few bigwigs. They decided to have some fun with him, so they had his brain transplanted into a maggot-dog."

Michael shrugged. "Okay, that explains it."

"And you?"

"I told you. I came here to find you. I wouldn't mind a drink if you've got one."

"I think we'll go out and have one. I'd rather not be a sitting duck in this apartment." She stood up and went to a plastic bag, from which she dug out another wig for him and a change of shirt and trousers. "Put these on."

While he was kitting himself out, she took a syringe and injected herself. Twenty minutes later they were sitting on the wall of the promenade staring out over the darkening sea whilst smoking cigarettes and swigging from a bottle of red wine. He watched her profile for a little longer than he had to. She didn't turn her head, just sat quietly and consented to being scrutinized.

"Those guys in your apartment? Are they working for you?"

She swung round and said, with ferocity, "Are you interrogating me?" There was a lull, just long enough for Janine to glance up and down the promenade and then discreetly inject herself again before refocusing on Michael, with a raised eyebrow.

"In case you think I'm a drug addict, I should make it clear I'm not. And I'm not into sex either."

"No drugs and no love. What do you live for, then?"

She looked straight at him for the first time. "I live for *nothing*," she said. "And it works just fine for me."

"In the long run we're all dead. Who said that?"

"Fuck Keynes and whatever he said. Fuck Hitler, fuck Mussolini in his pressed uniforms, fuck Stalin and his vodka and moustache, fuck the paranoid Zionists and their hatred for the Arab, fuck fucking Milton Friedman, fuck postmodernism, fuck the Nobel Prize. Fuck Mahatma Gandhi and fuck the Chinese, fucking yellow-bellied *naïfs* with their love of dollars, fuck the bandana warmongers with their AK-47s, fuck Tony Blair and his entourage of middle-class masturbators, fuck Sarkozy and his tight-assed out-of-tune wife... " She stopped. "I'm a student, that's what people don't get about me. And a sister."

"A sister?"

"Of God, my friend. Of God. Ever heard of Mary Magdalene?" Janine cut herself short and smiled at him. "What's *your* poison?" she asked. "You seem to think it's alcohol, but that's too brutal for you, Michael. I have a feeling your poison is religion."

"I'm not religious."

"Doesn't matter. I'd put money on it. That's your poison."

"You've had too much heroin."

"Probably." She looked at him, weighing it all up, then took the plunge. "Ever been to Sardinia, brother?"

"Now you're asking me questions."

"You want to come?"

"What for?"

"I know some nice people in Marseilles; they cut me open with a razor blade, put about five kilos of heroin inside me. They pay well. And they give you false papers." She stared hard at him, as if to impress on him the importance of such things.

"Did you know, Michael, there are hundreds of people in France like you and me?"

"I didn't."

"Our life expectancy is around two years. Most go to the doctor and get killed off. The rest try to stick it out, spread the seed around, pander to the little black-heads… then they die anyway. A very small elite end up doing what I do."

He noticed her use of the word "elite"—there was an element of pride in it, and self-inflation.

"What *do* you do?"

"You're very lucky, I think I'm going to show you. Because of Ariel and Günter."

That night they slept like brother and sister in her bed, in her blowup room—their dawdling hosts pacified by their high intake of heroin. In the morning they shared a cup of tea and a banana, then sat quietly thinking for a few moments, smoking a pack of cigarettes between them.

Midmorning a man in a dirty tracksuit came to photograph Michael. He announced he'd be back later with a passport.

They spent the rest of the morning shooting up.

At midday the new passport arrived by motorcycle courier. Janine slit Michael's belly open. The courier, a hollow-chested asthmatic with a smoldering joint in his mouth, did not recoil at the sight of the churning sea of maggots. He placed a heavy-duty foil bag on top of the seething mass and unceremoniously slapped the skin back in place. Within minutes, Michael was sealed up again with no scars and no lumps. Just a perfectly flat stomach.

They got on a train to Marseilles, then took a cab to the towering ferry in the harbor. Michael stood with Janine on deck, watching the tiered city basking in the late evening glow. Everything seemed perfect and dead as the great humming ship slipped its moorings and glided out.

16.

Janine had booked a super-luxury cabin with a bedroom and separate sitting room. Ensconced in a comfortable if slightly plasticized sofa, they had a fine view of the sea through a big, salt-stained window.

To ease their passage, they had bought two bottles of Black Label, two of Courvoisier, two hundred cigarettes each, and more bananas. (Maggots have a liking for bananas—they're basic starch.)

After a calm night, the ship docked sedately the following morning, and they wasted no time in hiring a car and driving into Cagliari, where they made their delivery and walked away with more cash than Michael had ever seen. Apparently cash would no longer be of primary importance to him. It was nothing but printed paper to be stuffed into his wallet and carelessly flung about when he needed something.

Janine seemed in excellent spirits as they emerged from the slightly down-at-heel apartment block (having just transferred their contraband into the grasping hands of a small-time villain).

"Come on, mister," she purred at Michael. "I've already saved your life and made you a pile of money; now I'm also going to make you immortal. Which means a short trip to St. Helena to meet the Mama."

"The Mama? Who the hell is that?"

"Oh, just the greatest stoner this planet has ever known. Once you're with her you'll never have to ask yourself again who you are or what your life's about. She'll tell you."

"I should probably think about it," he said, remembering Günter's words about never trusting anyone.

"*The man who thinks, deceives his own desires.* Mama told me that."

Janine drove inland from the rocky coast by Olbia, skirting inactive volcanoes, threading through hilltop villages. They saw a great number of ruined stone towers, and Michael reflected that there must have been a great civilization here once, though its people had failed, somehow, for they were all dead.

Slowly the landscape flattened out as they reached the western shore not far from Oristano. Towards midday they arrived at a covered black gate, with surveillance cameras on both sides peering down at them.

They sat waiting until the gates swung open.

Three or four hundred meters down a winding drive there was a slight incline towards an expansive terra-cotta roof partially hidden behind juniper trees. On the other side, the sea's horizon lay stretched like a massive, slightly curved rim. The courtyard was neatly swept but the banks on either side of the drive were overgrown with knotty, climbing geraniums that were more like small trees.

The door opened ahead of them, revealing a statuesque black maid in a pinafore dress—an emanation of the old Dixie South, practically singing a cotton-picking song as she stepped aside and let them through: "Just in time. She's getting impatient."

Janine lengthened her strides. "And what's happening?"

"Not much. Elvira brought some fresh people up, she found them in Olbia; they're all hopelessly in love already. Engorged. They don't know what's going on, but they're up for an orgy." The maid turned round and gave Michael a pointed look. "Don't mind my getup," she said. "It's Mama's idea of fun. She likes to put people down."

As they followed the maid's hips down a long, padded corridor, Michael poked Janine in the side. "What is this place?"

"A convent."

"It doesn't seem like a convent to me."

"That's the thing…" she said, with a wink.

They walked into a circular room with a bamboo-covered ceiling. At the center of it, encircled by a large group of white-robed chanting followers, sat a woman, a hawk-nosed late-fifties apparition, thin as a wishbone with hair so tightly pinned back that it looked more like a swimming cap. Her protruding eyes revolved back into place in her skull as soon as she grew aware of them, and seemed to linger on him especially. Michael had the uncomfortable feeling that he was being summarized or reduced in some way, and when she spoke he was slightly nauseated by the fastidiousness of her presence:

"Ah good. Janine. I was waiting for you. I don't like to wait."

"I'm so sorry, Mama," said Janine with exaggerated politeness and flopped down on a cushion, motioning for Michael to do the same. "I found this stray in Marseilles, hounded by the police. We weren't followed."

Mama seemed to find this amusing. "Really, Janine. Someone is always following us, don't you know?"

"Well, yes, if you put it like that, Mama," said Janine, clearing her throat. "We delivered two kilos to a Russian client in Cagliari." She got out her bundles of money neatly held together by rubber bands and passed them across to Mama. Michael did the same. Mama casually weighed the dough in her hands, then threw it in a bag and called for the pinafore-wearing maid, who came across the cushions in her high heels and took it away.

When it seemed they could no longer bear the silence, Mama opened her mouth wide and began to chant once again in a plaintive voice:

Oh cruel world, for too long have we waited here, for too long have we felt the lack of you, the hollow of you.

*No love for us and no making of love. Lord, how can we
survive in this shadow?*

The congregation joined in:

*Lord, hear our prayer, feed our despairing hearts. Give
us peace now and tomorrow... Amen.*

Once the ceremony was over, the cant and ritual was immediately discarded. Mama Maggot stood up and clapped her
hands. "We break for tea!" she announced.

Twenty or thirty individuals—all waiting for this signal—
bounced to their feet and hurried off like pupils released by the
bell, flinging their white robes untidily into a small anteroom.
Michael and Janine followed suit.

They went down a wide corridor ending in big glass doors
sliding open automatically, then crossed a courtyard through a
wicket gate onto a walled terrace shielded from view in every direction but open to the sea. Here one could persuade oneself that
nothing else existed in the world but the clouds passing over and
the sea like a dark band between the white walls.

The terrace was in immaculate order.

There were cushioned chairs, teak tables decorated with
fresh-cut flowers, tea lights lowered into glass lanterns. There
was fine china, which must have been carefully collected by
a connoisseur. The tableware was strikingly elegant, perfectly balanced in the hand and solid silver. There was Sardinian
sheep cheese, also imported Stilton from Harrods and short-
bread biscuits from Fortnum & Mason and tropical fruits imported from only God knew where, guavas and horned mel-
ons and papaya and guarana berries. Raku-fired bowls, each
a small masterpiece in its own right, were filled with açai and
bergamot preserves or freshly churned unsalted butter, and
there were baskets of toasted white bread under starched, very
clean linen napkins.

By now, Michael was familiar with the tendency. If one must
live as a maggot, one's available pleasures are severely limited.

Everything one does must be calibrated for maximum pleasure. The guiltiest pleasure of all, of course, is to lose oneself in artificial stimuli. To this end there were sealed plastic bags scattered everywhere, each containing three syringes pre-loaded with the very finest pink Afghani heroin. The trick was to dose oneself until a small portion escaped into the brain, inducing a pleasant high lasting no more than ten or fifteen minutes. After that, the maggots pushed out the toxins.

Even as they were settling in, he saw the deranged figure of the Mama, sitting to one side on a sort of throne at the edge of the terrace. She was in a world of her own, her hooked nose fixed like a compass needle on the setting sun over the sea.

Every half hour or so, a group of attendants with sponges and bowls of hot water entered the compound. Gently they undressed the dozing people and swabbed them down. The heroin, forming a glistening film on their skin, had a sticky quality, like crystallized honey.

"It's all recycled," Janine whispered. "Everything is recycled here, even people…"

Michael was too tired to ask her what she meant by that. He returned to his hut farther down the slope, where, if he opened the window, he could hear the waves lapping against the rocks below. The bed was crisp and comfortable, and when he lay down he noticed that also this ceiling was made of split bamboo canes. There was a shelf of books by American beatnik writers: Neal Cassady, Jack Kerouac, Allen Ginsberg, Lucien Carr. He leafed through a book by Allen Ginsberg, then threw it at the wall. It landed with the sleeve photograph of the poet with his big black beard and melting eyes staring at him and his smooth voice in Michael's ear:

> *Be cool, man, be kind to yourself, you're repressing it kiddo, I don't know what you're repressing, you oughta just feel it and do it… you know? Feel it and do it, in that order. You know why? Because you're okay, that's why.*

No sooner had his words guttered than Michael felt a smoke of heavy drowsiness lifting him, almost levitating him off the bed slightly, so that he lay there hovering. His mind was pleasantly distended. Sleep! For the first time in many days the maggots let their host lose himself.

At some point in the night he was awoken by a click of the latch, the door creaking and the weight of someone sitting down at the foot of his bed. There came a whisper: "Are you awake?"

"I am *now*."

He turned on his bedside lamp and saw a young woman sitting there, about twenty years old, more or less a carbon copy of Sophia Loren, only slightly less buxom.

"Yes. I know," she said. "I'm eye-candy, but who cares? God gave me my looks for nothing. And what's the real advantage of being good-looking, anyway? All that happens is you get guys swarming all over you until you can't tell the rotten apples from the good."

"I suppose you must be Elvira?"

"Yes, I suppose I must be." She hung her head, then added, "*By their deeds shall ye know them.*"

Michael cleared his throat, slightly guarded. "Sorry, but what are you doing?"

"I came to see you. I thought I could talk to you. Is that so wrong?"

He shrugged. "I guess it's okay. To be honest I don't know what to make of this place. What is it? Where are you from?"

"Oh, *nowhere*." Elvira pouted like a child deprived of her will. "Rome, of course. Everyone's from Rome. I never thought I'd end up serving some old bag who pinches my butt and makes insinuations all the time. But I'm used to bitches. When my mother wasn't having her nails done or lunching with girlfriends she was on tranquillizers—it's just a polite word for drugs, isn't it? She never gave a damn about me."

Elvira shifted in the bed, pulling her foot up against her buttock. A good girl does not open her legs, Michael remembered his own mother used to say. Nor does she show a white gleam of cotton covering her fuzzed pudenda. As he lay there watching her, Elvira got out a piece of semi-melted chocolate and broke off a piece for him. "You know something, I actually *like* you. I was watching you earlier, you seem like a nice man, not completely sex-mad like all the others." She put the chocolate in her mouth, with a simpering look. "I never chew chocolate. I *suck* it, to make it last longer."

There was a pause. Baby talk, was that supposed to be sexy? Or was she just habitually seedy? Michael asked: "How old are you, Elvira?"

"Oh, old enough, you'll find," she said. "Old enough to do what everyone else does, only a hell of a lot better. Basically I go out and find fresh meat for Mama. I bring it back for her and they fuck it."

Michael reached down into his bag for a bottle of Courvoisier. He took a stiff gulp at it, then rolled himself a reefer.

Elvira continued: "Mama gives me hell all the time. She fancies me. She likes to be clear about it, she says I mustn't work up any feelings for her. As if I would. Feelings, what a lovely word. What does it really mean? Having feelings actually means you only care about yourself, your own precious emotions."

"So Mama's a lesbian?"

"No, she's a maggot woman; *that's* what she is. It's the old Sapphic dream, the Kingdom of Women, right? The problem used to be that lesbian women needed men so they could have children, hence the impossibility of an all-female world. Boys could be thrown in the river, of course, but they'd have to keep one or two. For breeding. But now women really don't need men anymore. With the maggot tank they can live for ever. They don't have to bother with childbirth."

"What's the maggot tank?"

"Mama says I have to treat her well, she says I'm not the only half-decent looking cunt in this world. I guess she's right. There are a lot of cunts in this world, Michael. Most of them are not worth bothering with." She stood up. "Put something on. She wants to see you; that's why she sent me here."

"To ask me to come?"

"To tell you."

17.

"I expect you're wondering why you're here?"

Mama Maggot, stooped in a high chair like an old and twisted parrot on its perch, seemed to hover above Michael, who found himself semi-reclined in a leather armchair, blinking up at her face.

She looked unassuming and reasonable and he knew he was supposed to believe that maybe she actually was unassuming and reasonable. Except he didn't believe it. She was acting, and actors have to make it clear what they are doing or they become sinister or just plain odd.

The room was refrigerated; their breath came out in puffs of steam. Mama Maggot luxuriated in a white fur coat, though her skinny pale legs stuck out at the bottom like sticks, which rather spoiled the effect. On either side of her stood a small girl also dressed in a white fur coat, balancing on gold-sequined high-heels. From time to time, if Mama Maggot grew agitated, one of them would totter forward and kiss her cheek to calm her nerves, and whenever this happened Mama Maggot would turn to the child in question and kiss her full on the mouth, whilst intermittently shaking her head in wonder and whispering, "Thank you, my child, thank you." As if their concern came from the goodness of their hearts.

Michael had only thrown on a cotton slip when he left his room. He was already shivering. "Do you mind my asking?" he began.

"Yes, I do mind!" said Mama Maggot, doing her best to maintain her benevolent smile. "You're to be quiet, I require nothing but two words from you and those words are 'yes' and 'no'. Just occasionally you may say 'I don't know.' Do you understand?"

"Yes."

"And don't talk to Elvira again. She's very mixed up."

"I didn't talk to her. She talked to me. There's a difference."

"To me you're nothing but a sack of glorified fertilizer, so shut up and don't try to impress me!" After her venom had spurted forth, she slumped with deflation and received a volley of little kisses. Then, to his amazement, she began to talk like a normal person. "The truth is I do love Elvira. She's a little miracle, the way she's made. Like a Swiss watch; everything works so well. But what good has it done me to love her?"

"I don't know."

"No. You don't know. When God looks down at you he sees a little man peering round at not much. Mr. Michael. What a tragedy is Mr. Michael. He meets Ariel, who's been sent out to capture a fool of his sort to bring back here. Then she dies in shame. And Mr. Michael meets Janine, a stupid little self-propelled cunt tiptoeing about fearing for her pathetic life as if anyone cared whether she lived or died. As if it had any consequence. But at least the self-propelled cunt does as she's told. She brings Mr. Michael here. And now we are going to teach him. Do you know what we are going to teach him?"

"No."

"That's right, you don't. We are going to teach him to do our bidding. And stay alive until we say he should not be alive. I am responsible for you and many others; I am not autonomous. I must cull the lambs and I must lop the branches of the trees. Not by my own choice, but for the good of my community."

"Yes," said Michael, although he didn't much understand what she was talking about.

"Janine brought you here for a reason. She was told to bring you and she brought you. Now I have you. Do I have you?"

"Yes…"

"You are a fairly competent liar and this bodes well. With time you will improve; we will remove your scruples. Emotion is nothing but self-glorification. You will not suffer from that sort of rubbish; you will be a clean person. You will not be looking for self-advancement or personal power or in other words the workings of the ego which is the twisted impulse at the evil core of corporeal humanity. The world is doomed, you are doomed, even I am doomed; we are doomed by time so we may as well jig our bones about and feed our appetites. Do not come here speaking of goodness or charity. These things are for the lambs; these things are sparks rising from the fire, but the wind scatters them."

"Yes."

"The wheat is all chaff; we must eat chaff because there is nothing else. We like you, Michael. We like your puzzlement. You are weightless and empty like cheap white bread. Ariel liked you, too. She was told to find a lost sheep. A simple thing, you might think, but there are not quite as many lost sheep around as one might assume; one does require a little intelligence to go with the confusion. An intelligent human who is lost, that's an unbeatable combination. And Janine succeeded in this, at least."

He was silent, resentful.

"Yes."

"We need broken people to do our work; we need broken beings willing to do bad in the name of good. And if they are not already broken we are quite willing to do that bit for them. That is the name of the game, my little man. The church is about making moral judgments, nothing else. It can hardly ever be easy. And how can we be moral if the very fabric of the world is a blasted shroud in which we wrap ourselves? You must learn to see that all things are evil even if they seem good."

She pressed a switch. With a humming sound, a large glass tube rose smoothly out of the floor, until she sat entirely encapsulated within. The two pixies at her side had stepped away; there would not have been room for them inside. One of them fetched a bulky silvery gun, which she fitted into Michael's frozen hand. He could hardly bend his fingers and the metal was so icy to the touch that it stuck to his skin.

The cold had got to him. Not only the cold of the room, but the coldness of her words, the cold realization that Ariel had sought him out, had picked him for all the most unedifying reasons. He had put his foot into the noose she had held up for him with the very same forced smile he was seeing now, plastered extravagantly across Mama Maggot's face.

"In case you get the measly idea of trying to shoot me, please be informed that this is a bulletproof screen," said Mama Maggot.

The other girl fetched a Labrador puppy. She patted its golden yellow head and put it down on the floor, where it started flopping about and prancing playfully. Michael looked at Mama Maggot and somehow it did not surprise him that her smile had grown even sweeter.

"This is a very inconsequential exercise, Michael. But I love it more than any other. It is a sort of demonstration. An inversion. In a moment you will kill that thing. You will point your gun at it and you will pull the trigger. Why, you might ask yourself? Why do this to a little innocent thing only just setting off on its journey through life?"

Michael decided that his available list of retorts would not do, so he kept his eyes on the old bag and waited.

"Because this little thing is an illusion, Michael. In fact it is an evil thing, a brutal thing with no morality, no soul. It absolutely must be killed."

"No."

"Oh, but you will do it. You will not like doing it, but if you fail to do it I shall instruct one of my little ones to impale your brain…" She nodded to his left and Michael saw that one of the fur-coated children had raised a long spike towards the top of his neck, holding a little bronze mallet in the other with which to drive it home. Her tiny face had taken on a concentrated quality, and he realised this must be one of her special skills, something she had been schooled to do.

The tip of the spike certainly looked sharp enough to penetrate bone and effortlessly slide through a soft sack of membranes.

"Now that your training has begun you will be expected to kill a great many of these cute little things, Michael. You will be surprised at yourself. You will learn to accept it. You will learn to sleep easy in spite of all your disgusting deeds."

He glanced nervously at the twisted child behind him, worried that she might take the initiative. It probably would not hurt very much, he reflected. There would be a very brief pain that was not really a pain, more like a high-energy particle beam blinding one. Great pain overwhelms the senses, he had read somewhere. The small troubles of life, a grazed knee, a broken tooth, a scratched retina, these were the painful things. But a skewer through the brain might even be pleasurable, if handled expertly.

Michael raised his gun and considered the possibility of disobeying her and giving up the ghost. In the end he listened to a deeper, protesting voice telling him to do what she said. Was this the selfish ego she had spoken of, prompted by fear?

The barrel was equipped with a silencer. It made hardly a noise, only a sort of thud that he recognized from countless American films. It was much easier than he had thought.

The soft-nosed bullet shredded it utterly, leaving a trail of blood and gore. One moment there was a puppy there, jumping about. And then there was no puppy.

As soon as he'd fired the weapon and completed his task, one of the fur-robed girls tottered up to him and took his weapon away.

With a hum, the glass tube sank back into its recess in the floor. Mama Maggot stood up. "And so, Michael, now it is time to ask ourselves the question; is it more painless to die cleanly than it is to live in pain?"

"I don't know."

"Oh, but I think you are beginning to learn. I didn't know you were such a good boy, Michael. I suspected that I would never see you again outside this room. I suspected it." She smiled as if she was pleased that she'd be seeing an awful lot more of him. Pursing her lips, she continued: "*I don't know what you're repressing, you ought to just feel it and do it… you know? Feel it and do it, in that order. You know why? Because you're okay, that's why.*"

When he heard his own words repeated to him, he looked up and was properly afraid for the first time.

18.

After a few days of training, Michael was again woken one night at about two or three. Janine was standing over him, insistently shaking his shoulder.

"What *is* this place?" he grumbled. "The house of no sleep?"

"You're not shooting dogs tonight," said Janine with a troubled gaze.

Nervously he put on a clean white robe hanging on the door, then followed her outside. Dim solar powered lamps marked out the path down to the main house, but Janine climbed the hill and he followed without question.

Fifty meters below, they could make out the lit-up, screened-off terrace, where an orgy was in process. A band was playing flutes, sitars, cymbals, and tabla drums.

"So these five people have been tricked? They're being maggotized?" he said.

"They're being co-opted, yes."

"Is that *kind*?"

"Kind." She stared at him, shaking her head at his baffling stupidity. "I don't think your training is working. What kind of sugar-coated Disneyland do you live in?"

"I think it's just called normal life."

"Ha! There's no normal life for you, my friend. Not anymore."

"I'm not your friend. And you're not mine. Not after what you did to me."

"What did I do?"

"You brought me here."

They smoked in silence, watching as the Tantric ceremony below reached its apogee, with wails and frantic drumming. "I suppose," said Janine, who seemed to feel she had to qualify his accusation, "we all have to deal with our mortality, whatever we are: maggot people, flesh-heads, fuckwits, normals. We're all in the same boat. Look around you; look at the world full of people sleeping their way through life. When they die it scarcely matters because they weren't really born in the first place and they never opened their eyes. You're awake, you could try to be happy about it. And I'm wide awake and I have no intention of dying."

"That's just selfish."

She stood up and stubbed out her cigarette. "Idealist. Come on." She led him down the hill.

"Where are we going?"

"Sorry. She asked for you," said Janine, racing backwards into her obscure universe of self-justification.

They came to a circular stone building without windows. Mama Maggot was standing outside. She took a key from her pocket and unlocked a sturdy wooden door leading into what looked like a brewery. There was a large metal tank with a thick Perspex cover and a system of pipes and filters leading up through the ceiling. The tank was full to the rim with white, churning maggots. Beyond the faint hum of generators and fans, one could just about make out the slight hissing sound of their bodies rubbing together.

Michael shivered: he would have liked to pour gasoline on them and torch the little bastards.

"Hear that?" said Mama. "In spite of all your aggression, your hatred and your vengeance, I'll explain it to you. This is actually the song of the maggot. Shakespeare knew it well. He eulogized

the maggot; it was the great leveler to him. He referred to it as
the worm; did you know that?"

"Sort of," said Michael.

"To Shakespeare the worm was always a symbol of what lies
beyond. And the ultimate meaningless of anything we try to do
on this Earth. Whether we're kings or paupers there will always
be a worm waiting for us, even from the very moment of our
birth. You, for instance; as usual your mind is absorbed with self-
importance. But do you have any idea of how long you are des-
tined to stay here among us?"

"No one does."

"That's right. No one does. Only I know. I know how much
time should be allotted to everyone and that is why people do
what I tell them to do. I make a judgment on their viability."
Her fish-eyes revolved as she chuckled and held up a key. "In our
group we refer to this as the *passepartout*, the master key. Shall
I show you why?" She smiled with genuine amusement. "For
goodness sake don't be so afraid, Michael; it's only your little life
at stake, your little ego. The world will still be here after you've
gone." He felt his hackles rise, but before he could say anything,
she put her hand on his wrist and squeezed. "If you want to live,
Michael, do what I say. And don't use bad language…"

"I didn't say anything."

"Bad thoughts are a hundred times worse than words and
you are a very transparent sort. Also a very lucky one. You're due
for renewal and I'm going to give it to you."

"Renewal?"

"Shut up," said Janine. "Listen to her."

"There's a cycle," said Mama. "So we've learnt to breed the
maggots and keep them in perfect condition." She walked over to
the vat and peered inside with an expert eye. "This batch is perfect. Very young and pristine, very healthy, with a life expectancy
of around fifteen years. Are you interested, Michael?"

He flushed. "I'm not getting this. What do I have to do?"

She grabbed him by the neck. "Look, my friend. I've got the measure of you, I know how to determine a person when I see him and you don't have much time, you've used up too much of it with all your narcotics and drink. In a month or two they'll stop moving inside you and then you'll be gone. Why do you think Janine is still alive?" She looked across at Janine, who grew pale. "Because she does what we say and we reward her."

There was a long silence with nothing but the indistinct hissing from the vat, which seemed to be growing in intensity. Michael peered over at Janine, standing to one side with her face deferentially turned to the ground.

"So. What I'd like you to do now is undress and come here."

Janine whispered urgently: "Hurry up!"

Michael took off his robe and left it folded on the floor.

To one side of the vat was a strange adjustable rack, with two padded, curved prongs that fitted comfortably round one's neck. Michael reversed into it, and Mama adjusted the height of the prong so that it held his cranium tightly. There was a metal-tipped nozzle attached to a heavy duty rubber hose, which she sprayed with some sort of lubricant, then fed it unceremoniously into his anal cavity.

"What a nice uncorrupted young man." Mama sniggered at Janine. "His sphincter's like a rubber band…"

A machine was turned on—like a vacuum cleaner. He felt his innards gently sucked out until he hung there by the neck like a rag doll. Within seconds his brain grew light and ethereal and he sensed the eternal emptiness whispering at him. Through his fatigue and desperation he saw Mama's face looming before him.

"Now tell me you love me," she said. "Tell me you love me and I will hold that as a mark of your allegiance."

Michael tried to open his mouth, but the muscles refused to work. He managed to push some air out and make a croaking sound, which seemed to satisfy her though she took her time about it and raised her eyebrows pointedly as she made her way over to an instrument panel and flicked a switch. A bubbling stream of maggots filled him, maggots fresh and bursting with life; maggots intent on breathing, feeding and propagating.

Michael opened his mouth and took a breath, like someone surfacing from under water. "Thank God," he said.

"You have to thank Mama for the life you have," Janine corrected him, with a servile look at her mistress.

Once he'd been refilled, Mama checked a gauge to make sure the pressure was correct, then pulled out the nozzle.

"Now for the cakes and ale, dear boy. You must spend the night with a meat-girl and induct her. We've kept one by for you and you have to lie with her tonight. If you don't, you won't survive. You're stuffed with vibrant new maggots intent on life and they'll have what they want even if you do rather make a point of avoiding your own desires."

He wanted to run at her and beat her with his fists, then stamp her into the ground.

For the first time, Mama Maggot seemed to find his rebelliousness amusing. She had a slightly magisterial tone: "Listen carefully now. Injecting yourself with heroin won't help at this point; they're far too libidinous. So stay off the dope for a few days."

"This is a bloody disgrace."

"Oh, no doubt about it," said Mama, with a wry smile. "Except there's no blood with us. We're not fans of the stuff. We're the keepers of the life force, my little man. You may be a giver of roses but you forget roses also have thorns." She looked at him almost with affection. He noticed she had a very upper-class English accent, which came out particularly when she grew verbose. "Anyway, we gave up on grace a long time ago."

"I can see that."

"And you should, too. There is nowhere else to run, no more quaint notions for you. The perfume has run out, my little fool. You must come and show me what you've got; you must drop your pants, my dear, and reveal your equipment. Lead on if you please." She maintained her clawlike grip on his neck as she opened the door for him then shepherded him out into the brightening morning. "It's time for pudding…"

19.

Inside the enclosure, the Tantric orgy had descended into sedate conversation and herbal tea-drinking. Entwined, temporary lovers now waited for the sun to rise over the sea. In the windless air, acrid cannabis fumes hung over their bubbling water-pipes.

The Buddhists, of course, had not yet realized the Earth-shattering implication of their lovemaking. They felt themselves at home among these hospitable and libidinous strangers, this lavish complex by the sea with servants and even a plentiful supply of weed brought by a wisecracking black maid who, during the night's revels, had also revealed herself in her full vigor. One or two of the men had never before had sex with a black woman, and, to their surprise, had found she was much the same as a white one—undeniably with the same anatomy, although there was a kind of power in her haunches, a heat that spoke (to their projecting minds) of thousands of years of burning African sunlight.

But when the reed screen slid open to reveal Michael standing there in ceremonial robes, the Buddhists looked up with a slight sense of trepidation. Surely the amusements were over and done with?

Maggot Mama pulled the robes off his shoulders and let them fall in a heap to the floor. There was a sense of dismay among the Buddhists, which rapidly turned to relief when it grew clear that they were not expected to participate in what followed.

Michael was led very slowly towards a young Sophia Loren lookalike in the corner—Elvira—who, at the beginning of the night's revels, had single-handedly extracted orgasms from the three men and also fired up the three women with deep kisses and dexterous handiwork. The rest of the group had sat thoughtfully watching her expertise as if it were a performance of rare art. Which, in a way, it was.

In spite of her willingness earlier, Elvira was reluctant to participate. She held out her hands defensively. "Please! No, Mama." Something in her voice made them fearful. There was a plea in it, a timbre that connected them to the ancient fear of dying. "I'm sorry, Mama. I love you, I really do love you utterly, Mama. Without you I'm nothing."

She sank down on a cushion and started to cry. Mama nodded at her followers. Elvira's light cotton tunic was removed. By now she was limp and weeping uncontrollably, her face creased with pain and anger. But she was picked up by strong arms and positioned in a leaning stone chair at the edge of the terrace, with a narrow ledge for the buttocks and leather straps on the armrests and at the base of the legs. In no time at all she was secured in the contraption, her legs prized wide apart so that she immodestly revealed herself.

The Buddhists snuggled together, trembling and asking themselves how they came to be here in this place, among these people they did not even know?

Mama walked up to Elvira. Cupping her hands, she could not resist nibbling her luscious little earlobes one final time, whilst whispering audibly: "Prometheus, the rider with his lance, you must have seen him in the paintings? He does not ride out to kill the monster, my darling girl. Prometheus does not save you. He is not the prince. He is the monster and you are the sacrifice. Do you understand?"

"Oh, shut up, you crazy old lesbian! I don't know what the hell you're talking about!" screamed Elvira with all the force she had left in her lungs. Mama Maggot pulled back abruptly, her ears ringing. Then she motioned for Michael to be brought forward.

He, meanwhile, was almost swooning, shifting his weight from foot to foot. His body was bloated like a gammon left overlong in brine, and he felt the maggots swarming against the outer reaches of his brain. By some preternatural ability the maggots seemed to be sensing what was about to happen. They moved ferociously inside him; making it clear to him that if he did not steer himself towards Elvira—if he did not allow them passage —he would be burnt up and consumed. He took one step, then another—like a prisoner walking the plank with a sword poking into his back. Even his eyes were pushing outwards, as if about to pop out of his skull.

Elvira pleaded with him, but there was no way back for him. Strangely enough he felt no remorse as he quickly moved closer to her and without a second thought plunged into her and— while Mama's lips murmured into Elvira's ear—spent himself. His spasms repeated again and again until he thought he'd die with the exertion of it—continuing for as long as it took the sun to rise, spreading an oily redness over the spent waves, rising and falling indecisively like aimless afterthoughts.

20.

The next morning, after hanging around for as long as he dared on the beach, angrily throwing stones, he sneaked into the canteen, where he saw Elvira in a hooded black robe. She was sitting in a corner with Janine. Her skin looked very pale, and as he drew closer he realised it was because she'd been dusted in wood ash. Her hair had been shorn; her scalp was pockmarked and sickly gray.

As soon as Elvira caught sight of him she turned away, making it clear that she had no wish to speak to him. Janine stared at him. "It's okay, Michael," she said in a flat, expressionless voice. "She knows it wasn't your fault. But she doesn't want to speak to you. Anyway, you don't need me anymore; you have to listen to others who are more important than me. I'm just a courier, Michael; I thought that would be good enough for you, but apparently not." She paused, frowning at Michael, who stood there overwhelmed by the awfulness of what had happened last night. "Just go. Spare us the theatrics."

At the other end of the canteen, Mama Maggot was holding court to two high-ranking police officers in uniform and a delegation from the Vatican fronted by a cardinal in purple robes. When she noticed him hovering by the hot drinks counter, Mama waved Michael over and introduced him. Monsignor O'Hara was a tall, slightly stooped Irishman, his silvery hair shot through with insipid streaks of yellow. There was a fixed, glazed leer on his face: a sense of outrage, also an unwholesome fascination with the absurd—to him, all things that were not his own thoughts were a huge absurdity.

"Ah, so here he is, the fellow you've prepared for me."

O'Hara picked up his briefcase and shambled off towards the sunbaked terrace overlooking the sea, apparently expecting Michael to follow him. He spoke grandly and remotely, though with a lilting Irish accent.

"Wonderful place you have here. There's something almost Homeric about these waves, the way they wash in all pure and selfless. Christ would have lived here. Christ would have understood this. What a pity we cannot dwell on such things, what a pity we must concern ourselves with *finalities*."

They sat on a stone bench. Just ahead of them the volcanic rocks plunged steeply into the sea and shoals of glittering fish moved lazily through the green-blue depths.

As soon as their refreshments arrived, O'Hara tucked into coffee and biscuits and figs, making smacking noises as he sucked his fingers. His gold crucifix glittered. All the while, his shrewd, sick gaze lingered on Michael as if analyzing his every nuance. There was not a trace of self-consciousness about this examination—only fevered desire bursting out of him like bats spilling out of a cave—desire for the fulfillment of his purpose, whatever it was.

"Do you mind if I ask you a question?" said Michael cautiously. "Why are you here? What would a cleric want with us?" He felt his voice becoming tremulous when he spoke. O'Hara seemed pleased about his question.

"Do you think you are so evil that you're beneath our attention? God is concerned with all things, God is in all things, even in you." O'Hara's absentee smile returned, full of delight at this mental game, and noting with satisfaction that Michael was at a loss.

"Actually, yes. I think I am evil," said Michael after thinking it through. "I think we all are. I think we forgive ourselves and excuse ourselves. But, based on what I've seen, also what I've done… I'd say there's something evil at work here, and it's actually inside of us."

"Of course. Any fool can see that," said O'Hara. "Any goodness down here must fight a long, hard battle to win through. So don't judge yourself so hard in spite of the shameful things you have done. Consider a little more your actual survival in this place. I assume like most people you have a desire to continue breathing the sweet air of this planet and walk barefoot in the grass and wake up in the mornings?" He stopped for a finely weighted pause. "Where do I begin, talking to someone who knows so little? There has always been a maggot element in the Vatican, almost from the first moment the blessed Baptist started walking the hills. But there's rivalry between us and the flesh-bound priests. They don't much like us, though we can't see what's so special about them just because they have hearts and lungs and stomachs and theoretically the freedom to procreate, which we don't. We're regulated in the downstairs department," he added jauntily, then stopped and resumed his perusal of the waves. "But I'm surprised that you should begin by asking about me. Are you not more concerned about yourself, your own existence?"

"Not really," said Michael. "I'm rapidly losing interest."

"Very astute of you. Losing interest is often the best way of getting on in the world. Because you're no longer taking things so damned seriously. People like you have to learn to catch a decent wind when it comes along. And get those damned sails up." He glowered at Michael across the bony ridge of his wavering nose. "Because if you miss it, you could be stuck here for a bloody long time. In fact you may never leave at all. And between you and me," he whispered, "this place is just a coven of hags."

Michael sighed. "It is."

O'Hara nodded. "Excellent. Common ground is always welcome. But I can get you out of this place; I can give you freedom. Would you like that?"

"Yes," said Michael, forgetting his misgivings. "How?"

"We're having some problems, in the form of a flesh-head, an abbot outside Barcelona. A disreputable type. He's threatening to spill his guts, tell the world about the maggot."

"Why? What's he hoping to achieve by it?"

"Why?" The outrage on his face redoubled. "My word, what a question to ask! Let me see now. First I suppose he's embittered and second of course he's full of self-importance. He's been overlooked, he feels slighted. This way he can hold us to ransom in the name of morality." O'Hara shook his head disapprovingly and moistened his lips with sweet wine. "I'm going to tell you something, Michael, because I see promise in you, and I can respect that. This Elvira, who you supposedly deflowered last night. She's been a maggot for years."

"I don't think that's possible."

"It's an old trick and you're a very young man. They deflated her beforehand, she was nigh on half-full; that's why they tied her to the stone seat; she could hardly stand on her own two legs. Then you came along. But you never transformed her; the work had already been done for you." O'Hara leaned forward and shook him hard by the shoulder: "These people are playing with your mind, for what purpose God only knows. I don't seek to do that. All I am saying to you in a very straightforward manner is that there is something I want you to do for me. Unlike them, I don't want to destroy you or use you or steer your steps. I have work for you, it's as simple as that." He stopped. "There's some danger involved, I admit it, but the rewards are great. Afterwards you can go overseas. We'll furnish you with money to keep you ticking over."

Michael focused his energies. "What exactly would you have me do?"

"Ah yes." He put his briefcase on his lap and unlocked it, then took out a pistol with a silencer, which he pointed at Michael's face. "I want you to go to the offending Abbot. I will have you furnished with letters of recommendation from Rome. He will have no choice but to take you on as a novice. When you get the chance you put a bullet in his head. If at all possible, get your hands on as many of his documents as you can, which may be rather difficult as he's bound to have them secreted or locked away in strongboxes. Search his quarters, search his office. Oh, and don't concern yourself about the police. Once the Vatican machine finds out he's been murdered all the details will be duly covered up; that's standard practice." He paused. "Have no fear of divine recrimination, either. We've all agreed it's the only thing to be done, and you have absolution."

Michael sat still, listening to the waves.

I'll slip away when they're not looking, he told himself. I'll play the innocent but I'll do what they say. Afterwards I'll go to the Greek islands. I've got fifteen years of life left in me; I'll fish and sleep in a cave and then when my time's up I'll swim out and drown myself.

His reverie faded and he was aware of O'Hara waiting for his response.

"Sure," said Michael. "It's easy. I just pull the trigger, that's all."

The Cardinal held the gun under Michael's nose. "Keep pulling it until the target looks like a shredded puppy."

21.

Almost before he knew it, he was in an air-conditioned coach crunching across the gravel, leaving St. Helena behind. He'd been given a full collar shirt and cassock to wear, and they were quite unbearable in the heat. But as he sank into his seat and the cool air streamed over his flaming red face, he felt an overwhelming sense of relief.

The brothers and sisters of St. Helena in their sandals and white cloaks had come to wave them off.

Mama, standing at the head of the assembled group, had put on a colorful embroidered belt to set her apart. Elvira stood beside her, dressed in gray now to indicate she was close to blooming. Three white doves, attached to her by long red silk ribbons, pumped their wings frantically overhead as she strode forward ceremoniously, lifting her hand in a parting salute.

She seemed to be searching the coach's windows for him, and when she found him, her grave expression changed abruptly. She stuck out her tongue, taunting him, then held up a pair of golden scissors and cut the ribbons. The three doves rose into the sky, trailing their long red jesses.

Mama leaned forward and took Elvira's tongue into her mouth with tremendous greed.

Michael stared at the two women, deeply troubled by their inhumanity, also relieved that he would never have to see them again. Another thought struck him: maybe this was precisely what they wanted him to feel? Once a person is broken, he can be bent and twisted. A broken man is a mechanical instrument made of flesh. Hadn't Mama Maggot told him so?

He rested back in his seat, choosing not to talk to anyone, focusing his attention instead on the video screens showing Pope Innocent giving his benedictions, waving his white-robed arm over the assembled masses in St. Peter's Square.

The sea crossing and disembarkation in Marseilles were uneventful, but just before they reached the Spanish border, O'Hara told Michael he would be dropped off at the train station in Perpignan.

At about noon, the bus pulled into the small, dusty town and waited with its engine idling. Perpignan lay, as it has always lain, a conflicted settlement on an undefined border.

O'Hara walked into the station with Michael, clutching at his arm. Old ladies smiled fondly at these two saintly men so urgently engaged in conversation. Talking of God, no doubt.

They stopped outside the station café just as the Barcelona-bound train pulled in with screeching brakes like a many-armed serpent, North African immigrant workers hanging out of the windows, smoking and laughing, finally on their way home after months of undignified labor among infidel Parisians.

O'Hara gave Michael the address of a bar in the Gothic quarter of Barcelona, where a local crook by name of Sergio had a weapon for him to pick up. "A nice little Beretta," said O'Hara. "Should do you just fine. But do throw it away somewhere safe once you've finished with it."

He gave him a photograph of the abbot, a rotund and rather harmless-looking cleric. On the back of it was written the name of a monastery in Ripoll.

"He doesn't look too bad to me." Michael stared at the photo.

"Oh, bad enough, you'll find," said O'Hara, with a glare. "And you? Are you a good man, would you say?"

"If I was good I'd be dead."

"It's a good answer."

The Irishman produced an envelope from his pocket with an address scrawled on it. Inside was a set of keys. "Afterwards, lie low for a while. There's food in the fridge and plenty of stimulants. After about two weeks some men will come to pick you up. In the night."

"Pick me up? Or shoot me? Boil me? Or will you just stick to water-boarding?"

Michael rose from his seat and grabbed his bag, but O'Hara clawed his fingers into his arm. With a sinking feeling, Michael looked down at his yellow, filthy nails. "Don't cross me, Michael, I may have a crucifix round my neck but in essence I am a soldier. Don't forget it!" O'Hara softened his grip. "My friend," he said consolingly, "it's natural that you should resent me, but don't let this cloud your judgment. You will have to be quick and bright to rid us of this troublesome abbot. Be aware of the fact that he and his entourage will try to trick you. They'll be every bit as tricky as the horrendous maggot folk you just left behind. They'll know that you have Vatican authority for what you're doing. And they will play with your mind because that's what people do. People are liars. People are swine."

22.

A few hours later the train pulled into the reeking hinterlands of Barcelona. The moment Michael put his foot on the dust-swirling platform of Estació de França and walked into the bright and windy sunshine of the cocksure city, he felt as if his retinas and eardrums had been renewed. His senses came alive. With the ardors and strains of St. Helena behind him, he was like an exhausted mud wrestler stepping into a hot shower at the end of the day. And yet he also had a sense of a quickening inside, as if the maggots were aware of the task at hand and had decided to sharpen up their act to ensure his survival. Of course this was not because they cared about Michael, rather because they wished to preserve him. He was their country, after all. And so, technically speaking, he had a body that knew what to do.

After the many hours he'd spent in St. Helena poring over street maps, he was able to navigate without difficulty through a labyrinth of narrow streets into the old Gothic quarter. His body steered itself effortlessly, like driving a fast car. He stopped outside a dingy little bar which lacked even a sign above the door.

A dirty shower curtain over the entrance moved in the draft of the diseased airs from within. It was Sergio's bar, he assumed.

As he stood there watching, a woman built like a crane, with arms and legs thrashing in all directions came hurtling out of the doorway as if she'd been given a violent push from inside. She tore down the curtain on her way out and ended up on her miniskirted tail.

Instead of getting up she hauled out a packet of cigarettes and lit one with a philosophical frown. But her self-control was short-lived. "Fucker!" she cried, turning round. When no one came out, she stayed where she was on the pavement, calmly puffing on her cigarette.

Michael stepped forward. "I'm looking for Sergio."

"Oh, leave us alone!" she snapped. "I hate you people. Sergio hates you, too." Then, thinking about it, she added: "Sergio hates everyone."

He noted that she seemed to have a perfect East London accent and this filled him with a certain wistfulness. It also occurred to him that he was still wearing his vestments, hence the confusion. He got out his wallet, showed her some money and as a result stirred up even more confusion: "I could do with a bit of heroin; I'm gasping for it to be honest."

"Heroin?" The girl stared, her opinion of him rising slightly. "You want heroin? Lord fucking preserve us." She scratched her head. "I can't go back in there now, padre, he's gone fucking mad 'cause I won't lick up his spit."

"Excuse me?"

"He does that, the dirty fuck. He spits on the floor and I'm supposed to lick it up."

"And do you?"

"No! And then he fucking beats me. The fuck!"

"Maybe I should go and have a word with him."

A sliver of light entered her eyes, and she laughed, revealing a gap-toothed mouth. "Yeah, go on then, padre. Go in if you fancy a broken tooth; that's his specialty."

"I have some other business with him. Don't worry about me," said Michael, picking up the curtain and rigging it back onto the rail before he stepped in.

His eyes fell on a fat, beady-eyed gypsy woman behind the bar.

"Sorry," he said. "I'm looking for someone called Sergio?"

She nodded. "Why you sorry?" Then added, "Sergio not here," and pointed to a back door, whilst at the same time speaking a few words under her breath to a dark, sharp-chested youth of no more than seventeen, who ran off.

Michael sat down. The long-limbed woman came back in and sat down with him. He offered her a drink and she asked for a Cinzano with ice.

"What's your name?"

"Call me Honey," she said. "What kind of fucking priest are you, anyway? Did you bust out of a monastery?"

Michael downed his drink. "I'm the sort of priest who believes in doing whatever he likes."

"What's that, then? Girls or boys? Or either?"

"I like everything except what I don't like and I don't like anything. You understand?"

"You don't make a lot of sense to me but I won't hold it against you. One thing I know: if I just sit here I'll get another hiding when he comes back."

"Don't worry; I'll take care of it," said Michael.

Again she laughed and again that little streak of light entered her eyes. "You're crazy. You're worse than my mother."

"Your mother, what's she got to do with it?" said Michael, realizing that this was the key to her.

"Yeah, my mother. Don't you have a mother?" she said defensively. "Course you bloody do, everyone has a mother even if she's dead."

"Don't worry; mine's dead as well."

The peace was shattered when a bunch of tracksuit street sharks piled in behind an acne-scarred Andalusian gypsy. The sharp-chested youth passed something across to the gypsy woman.

"I guess that older gypsy guy is Sergio, right?"

"He's going to throw you out on your ass like he does with me," said Honey.

"Oh, he'll be all right once I've explained things to him," said Michael, with an assurance that even he found perplexing.

The fat gypsy woman came up and wanted fifty euro for two drinks. Michael paid up without protesting, which seemed to impress her. Quickly she asked for another hundred, then hitched up her skirt and gave him a cellophane-wrapped package from somewhere among her underwear. He got out his cash-fat wallet and paid. As he did so, he noticed Sergio sitting on a stool keeping his eyes on him before coming over. (Why is it that robbers always feel they have to start a conversation before they get to work?) Michael pre-empted him, walked up to him and grabbed his arm and muttered into his ear: "I've come for the Beretta."

Sergio reluctantly took his eyes off the pocket where Michael had put his wallet.

"Why you did not say?"

"Sergio, I could ask you things too. Why you don't do something useful with your miserable life? Why you prefer walking around with a turd stuck up your ass? One of these days you're going to shit yourself and then we'll all know about it. You'll stink to high heaven."

Honey couldn't believe her ears. Michael counted four missing teeth in her wide-open mouth. Nervously she began itching her arms, pulling up her sleeves and exposing countless track marks and infected hypodermic punctures.

For the sake of convenience Sergio decided to find the joke amusing. He roared with hoarse laughter, slapping his thighs. "Fucking God-man with no shit in your ass like a faggot, come back in an hour... I give you Beretta, okay."

Michael located a cheap hotel nearby, where he left his high-density plastic suitcase padlocked to the balcony railing. His room overlooked a narrow section of street fronted by cut-price electrical stores. Tall African men in colorful clothes stood haggling on the pavements or walked about with cardboard boxes (televisions, for the most part) balancing on their heads.

When he opened a little cabinet above the mirror, it was full of used syringes. He didn't have much time, just about enough to fix himself with one of his own needles and have some anchovy fillets on toasted bread and a glass of wine in a cavernous restaurant patrolled by gloomy waiters.

When he got back to Sergio's bar, the curtain was still undulating lazily in the draught but the place was much too quiet. He stood for a moment, letting the maggots do their surveillance.

They were decidedly uneasy, and he was learning to listen to them.

Just as he was about to step inside, he registered a movement in the window. The gypsy woman was crouching behind the aluminum-topped counter. Shielding his face with his forearm, he parted the curtain and stepped over the threshold directly into the path of a swinging baseball bat. His maggot arm bent out of shape from the impact, but with his other hand he lashed out, grabbed Sergio by the larynx and propelled him very hard into the concrete wall. His face made a nasty crunching sound as the bone and gristle separated. At the same time Michael felt a knife stabbing into his body from behind. The blade went in more or less directly where his kidney would have been, killing a good few maggots as it did so. Michael reacted instantaneously—or, more accurately, the maggots reacted.

He spun around and looked into the twisted face of one of Sergio's men who thought the job was done, but in a flash Michael had wrenched the knife out of his grip and opened up the brute's arm like a fish gut. Remotely, as if through a pair of broken headphones, he heard the poor man shrieking.

Sergio was squatting against the wall, pointing his flattened nose at the ceiling to stop any more shedding of blood over his dirty shell suit. His face had already ballooned. Michael could just about see the gypsy barmaid's head behind the bar, where she was sitting on a low stool presumably kept there for occasions such as this.

"While I'm waiting for my Beretta, I'll have a large whiskey, if you please Signora." Without getting up, her fat arm put a glass and bottle on the counter. Michael did his own honors and helped himself to a cigarette from an abandoned pack.

Ten minutes later the Beretta arrived.

"Take it, padre," said Sergio with self-righteous indignation. "If you come here again, I shoot you in the head."

"Are you crazy, attacking an honest man of the cloth?" said Michael. "Can you really look me in the eye and tell me this was not deserved? You want to go to prison? You want your ugly faces splashed across the national newspapers, you stupid pork-eating slugs? How much beer do you get through every day, how many cigarettes? Lose your fucking spare tires before your hearts give up. Go home to your women and children, if you have them. Take a look at yourselves—do something with your lives before it's too late!"

Sergio, looking to reassert some authority, barked at Honey. "You! Get me fried chicken!"

Michael took her arm. "Sorry. She's coming with me."

Sergio sniggered even as he winced: "I don't care. Take her, she almost dead and you almost dead too. If you come back here you dead, and if you not come back here you also dead. I am not a crazy. But I know you are a crazy, because you love a stupid bitch like she. Goodbye..."

23.

That night, Michael dreamed of Purissima, standing in her aromatic rose garden, looking anxious. She was calling to him, circling her nest like an alarmed blackbird as an intruder came crashing through the undergrowth.

He realized *he* was the intruder.

Up ahead he saw a dark tower with a single lit window. Inside, he saw Ariel standing with Sergio, who had just covered the floor in gobs of green snot and was pointing down and screaming at her to get on with it.

He checked his pistol, only to discover that the chamber was empty. The firing pin made an empty click. He was surrounded by guards wielding high-powered automatics. All took aim at him as he started running.

He woke to the sound of ricocheting bullets and lay there disoriented in the early morning light until he noticed Honey next to him in the bed—her yellow miniskirt like a dead butterfly on the dirty floor. In the early morning light her face was pale as powdered chalk. He did not disturb her as he got up and showered, keeping the door open to make sure she did not try to escape.

His body felt smooth and pleasantly enervated; his system was in balance. He lit a cigarette and ordered up coffee and pastries from the street, which he took at the door without letting the waiter inside.

He pushed away the thought of the abbot in Ripoll, the disgusting thing he'd been sent to do. Why not just take Honey and go into hiding somewhere far away? Live their short lives under the palm trees, fill their hut with squawking parrots and pink conch shells? Feed on fruit and the fish of the sea?

Honey woke up coughing. "Jesus, you smoke, don't you?"

"Yeah. I need cigarettes or I die."

She laughed and slurped her coffee. "I like you better like this, without those *puta madre* robes. Under all that nonsense there's a man, I can't see what's wrong with that. Personally." Her face clouded over and he saw her brittle wrinkles emerging. "I have to get back to the bar and give Sergio his money."

"Don't go back. You're safe here."

Honey reached down to pick up her dress and said in a forced, breezy voice: "You don't know much about girls, do you, padre? We like doing our own thing and we get bored easily." She smiled. "There again, the way you were going for it last night I could tell you hadn't had a pair of thighs round you in years." Her careworn body, covered in cellulite and folds of white pinched fat, filled him with a strange affection.

"You're lonely," she said. "Did your mother give you enough hugs when you was a kid?"

"I told you, my mother's dead."

"Yeah, but she wasn't dead when you was a child, was she?"

"No."

"Well then! Did she or didn't she?"

"I can't remember," he said. "Probably she did. But that's not important now. What's important is that you stay here; you mustn't go back to Sergio."

"Why not? He's a good enough bloke," said Honey. "Could be worse, anyway. He's not a mass murderer."

"Not yet. What about the spitting thing?"

"It's only spit. I've had worse." Her sharp features softened. "I know why you want me here with you. Shall I tell you?"

He nodded. After the mind-reading capabilities of all the maggots he had met, it was comforting to lie there next to Honey, whose deviousness seemed innocent as gamboling lambs.

"It's because you're surrounded by wankers. You've had 'em milling around you for a while. It took you a while to get it straight in your own mind, but now you're sure. They're wanky, no doubt about it, only you can't think of nothing to do about it because they've got loads of dough and they'll squash you just like that!" She clicked her fingers, then blinked at him eagerly. "Am I right?"

"Close."

"So we're the same. You and me are the same." Honey sat up and started wriggling into her panties. "I really have to get back to the bar. I got all my stuff there, Michael; I can't just leave, can I?"

"What fucking stuff? A pile of scuffed-up magazines? Broken ashtray? Couple of tubes of squashed lipstick? Some torn nylon miniskirts? Or what?"

"Yeah! It's my fucking stuff and I want it!"

"Wait! We haven't finished yet. And anyway I'm going to make you an offer. I'll personally take you out and buy you whatever you like." He stopped and let his words sink in.

"How much money you got, padre? What did you do, raid the collection box?"

He showed her his wallet, stuffed with O'Hara's hundred-euro bills. "I've got enough," he said. "You have to listen. You won't survive if you go back. Things are going to change for you very soon; you won't recognize yourself. What we did last night was a one-off. I'll never touch you again."

Honey had experienced this sort of thing before: life-weary, sometimes impotent men with money (or without) who wanted companionship.

"You're not getting me, mate. Sergio won't be happy about yesterday; you made him look a right idiot. I'd get out of here if I was you; he'll find you. We're not far and it won't take him long to track down a shambles like you, a fucking priest who don't even shave, sitting about with a pack of fags and a bottle of vodka. I'm telling you, the Barrio Xino aint big enough… and if he finds you he'll beat the crap out of me as well."

"I'll shoot him if he gets anywhere near us," said Michael, stretching out on the bed and lighting another cigarette. "I have a gun, you know."

"I've met a lot of crazy fuckers in my time, padre, but you really take the biscuit." She snuggled into the sheets and scrunched up her face. "It's weird but I do feel safe with you. If you keep me in drugs I'll stick around for a while. But I need clothes, man, I can't wear this fucking miniskirt any longer." She wagged her finger in the air. "Just don't get hurt, okay? That's a deal-breaker. And don't ask me to come down the fucking hospital if you get knocked about. I can't stand wasting time in those places. Medics checking you and telling you a load of shit and taking your blood. They don't know their face from their ass."

"What about you?" he said. "Did you get hugged enough?"

"To be honest," said Honey, "I never even knew what a hug was. To me it was just some bloke wanting to stick his cock in."

"And your mother, what happened to her?"

"I reckon that was where the rot started. If she'd been around I wouldn't have gone on the game. I met Sergio in Benidorm. I was down there for a holiday, sunning myself on the beach and enjoying a couple of pints with the girls. We had a good time back then."

"Then what happened?"

"I was only sixteen when mum died and then we lost the house. Mum didn't have any family 'cause no one liked her and they chucked her out. 'Cause she was on the game as well, you see."

"And Sergio treated you well?"

"Sergio put me to work and for the first time in my life I had some money. He's a fucking bastard but at least he survives. If some cunt comes along and gives him shit he beats the hell out of them."

"And you like that?"

"He's not a coward, anyway. I tell you Michael, if there's one thing I can't stand it's a coward."

"What was your mother like?"

"She was a sweetheart. I'll take her with me when I go. Oh fuck, now you're making me fucking cry! Anyway, it's all over now, nothing you can do. She was a poor thing, now she's a poor dead thing. Done is done. You only get one shot, Michael. After that you're done. One shot."

"That depends," said Michael. "My people reckon you get more than one shot."

"Your people are wankers, we already agreed about that," said Honey. "And even if they're right, even if you come back, you'll only end up doing the same bloody thing all over again. It's fucking karma; you don't get past it. How many times have I told myself I'll never pull some stunt again? I think I've learnt my lesson, but I never have learnt it. I keep fucking up. It just repeats itself and now I don't care anymore. I'm a loser but at least I can hold my head up. Because I can say I'm not a wanker."

24.

The new clothes Michael had bought for Honey made her feel like Grace Kelly. She tottered out of the Hostal Paradiso in a pair of mauve silk trousers, a leopard-print silk scarf, flouncy pink blouse, wide-rimmed hat, oversized sunglasses and so much rouge that you could have written your name on her cheek with the tip of your finger.

She crossed the street as if expecting all the traffic to stop for her, then collapsed into the waiting taxi where Michael sat nervously glancing at his watch. "God, this is not my idea of fun," she whined as she settled into the vinyl seats, crossing her bony kneecaps and plugging her glossy mouth with a cigarette. She lit it with a gasp, ignoring the protesting cab driver who finally gave up and lit his own. "I'd rather just stay in bed with a magazine."

Michael leaned forward to give their destination to the driver. "St. Joan de les Abadesses, Ripoll." He felt a searing pain hounding through him. For a moment he feared his maggots were dying until he saw that they had actually reflected back at him the wave of bleak emotion they had just sensed.

The clever little swine were learning empathy now as well.

Or were they just warning him, telling him to concentrate?

The taxi drove through the late evening rush hour, up the Via Laietana past the old Roman fortifications, then headed north out of the city through bleak industrial hinterlands, past stinking chimneys and cemeteries shaded by yew trees. Cities were like people—surrounded by inhospitable boundaries and densely compressed into small, trampled areas. In the end, he reflected, even the human personality became a sort of tourist destination.

Honey whispered softly into his ear that she could do with another hit. She had the soft insistence of a child. If she were careful about it, did he think she could shoot up without the cab driver noticing? Michael ignored her and tried to prepare himself for what lay ahead.

His feeling of disquiet did not leave him as the taxi exited the highway outside Ripoll and dropped them off in the town square. The balmy evening, the strolling people, the slumberous cafés: all seemed sinister to him. Michael looked at Honey, flouncing along with her ricotta limbs, making a spectacle of herself. Potentially, she was a bit of a liability, but there had been no alternative but to bring her. He had to do his duty by her—he could not abandon her to a short, painful, and miserable existence as a rogue maggot. He left her in a hostel, gave her a syringe, a foil parcel of heroin, a bottle of water, and a copy of *Vogue* and told her he'd be back soon.

After checking that his gun was clean and loaded as he'd been taught at St. Helena's, he made his way down a sunken lane towards the monastery. The intermittent sound of sprinklers on the front lawns was all that could be heard from the other side of the wall.

There was a small group of men by the gatehouse—tough-looking T-shirted fellows with short-cropped hair and tattoos on their stocky arms. Mainly out-of-work neo-Nazis by the looks of it, stuffed dolls held together by nails, rope, and empty rhetoric.

Michael showed his letter of introduction and explained that he had an appointment.

On their way to the main building Michael saw more security people secreted in the bushes. A glint of the dying sun caught the barrel of a gun. He was struck by a thought: O'Hara had never explained to him how he was supposed to get out in one piece.

By the front doors he found himself facing a large jovial monk who introduced himself as Brother Paolo.

"Welcome, Brother Michael." A stout, hairy arm reached out and shook his hand warmly. "We're all most pleased you got here in one piece…"

Michael frowned, remembering something Günter had said about a fat monk from Rome who used to give him sweetmeats. "Paolo? You don't know a man called Günter, do you?"

"Let me see? A man called Günter; no, I don't know *a man* called Günter, no, decidedly not."

An understanding passed between them. Michael could not quite understand how Paolo, a flesh-head, should be a good friend of Günter. It made no sense.

"Who are all these men in the grounds?"

"Oh, they were offered to us. Apparently we have a security scare on our hands. Some lunatic on the loose or something." Paolo led him into the bowels of the building as he spoke. "The trouble with guard dogs is you never know who they'll bite next."

"Who are they guarding?"

Paolo sniggered and turned round. "They said you'd be a joker."

"Who said?"

"Well. I imagine Cardinal O'Hara might agree. You saw him recently, did you not? In Sardinia?"

Michael felt himself suck air into his chest cavity, a mental reflex. Truth seemed the most sensible option, and he deployed it. "Yes. I did."

"Good. Thanks for being honest about it; that speaks volumes. Now follow me and I'll take you to Giacomo."

Outside the abbot's main suite there were more security men, frazzled unshaven brutes with cigarettes behind their ears and chunky rings on their fingers. The place smelt of cheap hamburgers or intestinal gas—that indistinguishable global perfume of the underclass. The brutes glared at him as he passed. He caught the unmistakable whiff of hostility.

The highly polished mahogany doors opened. Paolo waved him into the enormous, air-conditioned chamber beyond. Michael ventured in like a nervous ice skater gliding onto a glittering rink.

Paolo vanished and the doors closed behind him with a heavy clunk, followed by a sonorous click as the key was turned on the other side. He heard voices raised, a discussion on the other side: the sound of Paolo's booming affability and the growling opposition of the security men, who seemed to prefer to keep the doors unlocked.

For a while he stood there, unsure of himself. There was no sign of the abbot. To his right, a table with carved griffin legs looked ready to spring at him.

There was a crackling sound as if a microphone had been switched on and some muffled fidgeting. Then a fluid, confident voice with a clear agenda.

"Good evening, Michael. Do you know who Ignatius Loyola was?"

Michael looked round. The voice came from speakers all around, a sort of unnerving quadraphonic effect, an omnipotent intelligence coming at him from every direction. "Yes, I think I do," he replied at last. "Does it matter?"

"Does it matter?" There was a long-drawn chuckle. "Very good. So hear this. St. Ignatius Loyola, when asked how he would feel if the Pope suppressed the Order of Jesus, answered: 'A quarter of an hour of prayer and I should think no more of it.'"

There was a silence. Michael sank into a heavy, ornate chair. "I'm sorry, why are you telling me this? I don't even know who you are?"

"I am telling you this to explain the pitfalls of holding on to things. The satchel on your shoulder, my friend, is full of all the excrement you have squeezed out of your bottom from the day you were born; still saying goodbye to your bobbing little friends, are you not? Am I right?"

Michael clutched his head. "Do you know, the only person who tells me the truth is a heroin-using prostitute I met on the streets of Barcelona."

"Of course. The desperate have no agenda except to eat. Look, can I be frank with you? I can't stand another day of these Vatican-financed apes clogging up the place and oiling their blessed guns."

"Where are you?"

"Not within range of your fire stick, you can be sure of that. Do you think it's possible that Judas Iscariot *did* have God on his side? If so there might be hope for you."

Michael looked round the palatial room—the thick, four-meter-high curtains in the windows, the wainscoting, the rough gray floors without a speck of dust.

He touched the long, warmed barrel of the gun against his leg.

The voice kept talking: "See the mirror at the other end of the room?"

"Yes."

"Walk towards it unless you'd rather be gunned down like a wild hog by O'Hara's people."

"I thought all these men were *your* security people?"

"Oh dear Lord, no. They're Vatican personnel sent by O'Hara to finish you off, or both of us. It's a classic technique. Think of Lee Harvey Oswald—first kill the target. Use a simple guy; dupe him or threaten him in some way, then once the job's done get some deranged footman to bump him off."

"Why should I believe you?"

"You believe the one who tells the truth," came the answer. "'*Multi multa sciunt et seipsos nesciunt.*' It's Pseudo-Bernard: 'Many know many things yet know not themselves.' Very true, particularly of you, Michael."

"Now what?"

"Turn round, go back towards the doors. Stop by the first window. Good. Now look to your right. See that little painting of Joseph and Mary? Go there. Move yourself! Press the frame on the top left side."

Michael hurried over, pressed the frame and heard a click as the outline of a door revealed itself.

"Go through and close it behind you. They're coming through now."

At the other end of the room, a key was turned in the lock and the double doors started swinging open.

Michael slipped inside and pushed the secret door into place behind him as quietly as he could.

25.

"I should introduce myself. My name is Wizard. That's the short version. My full name is Wizard of Oz."

Abbot Giacomo leaned back in an ergonomic office chair and seemed to be enjoying his own joke. He was a portly man dressed in a beige, rough-spun alb girded with a cincture, the whole thing spectacularly stained with specks of oil and tomato sauce. His delivery was rapid and witty, like a forties movie star.

"Let's see, first things first and last things last. You've brought a weapon, I assume? Otherwise what the hell are you doing here?"

Awkwardly Michael got out his gun and put it on the table. He felt ashamed of himself.

Giacomo's eyelids fluttered disapprovingly. "You poor little dumb shit running round the world doing the bidding of disgusting flesh-heads." Using a small paper knife, Giacomo slit his skin enough to show a seething mass of maggot underneath, then said: "I am maggot. O'Hara isn't maggot. Do you understand?"

"Why would he do that? Come to St. Helena and go to such extreme lengths to fool people?"

"He didn't fool anyone. They all knew. There's a quota. The only one who was fooled was you."

"What quota?"

Giacomo sighed. "Where do you think St. Helena gets its money from? How much money do you imagine it takes running a place like that?"

"They sell drugs."

"Most of their money comes from the Vatican and in return they provide a certain number of specialists to Rome every year. Mainly assassins to deal with the odd difficult banker or heads of small African states or uncooperative tribal chiefs who resist progress. O'Hara recruits for Rome. It's generally acknowledged that maggot people make better killers. O'Hara must have liked you an awful lot, only he's not supposed to kill off people like me. He knows that. I'll give him a good deal of trouble for this."

"He'll deny it."

"Of course he will. But he's not the only clever bastard in the world."

"And I hope I'm not the only stupid one."

"Don't be so hard on yourself. You weren't to know."

"He said you'd be tricky. He said you'd try to fool me."

"Now you really are being a fool. He hates us maggots; it's a well-known fact." He paused. "Luckily for you, we were tipped off."

"Who by?"

"Günter. He made contact a few days ago from Rome to tell us he'd packed you off to Janine, one of the worst 'procurement cunts' in Christendom. That's in his own words, I stress. She pretends to be a drug dealer." Giacomo looked up. "So let me ask you something; what did you think of O'Hara?"

It was the first time in a long time that Michael had been asked anything at all as if his opinion mattered.

"I thought he was an unbearable shit. I suppose I just assumed anyone who's climbed to the top of the greasy pole has to be a bit of a bruiser."

"Or a very devout person, has that occurred to you?" Giacomo shrugged. "Let me ask you something else. Try testing your intuition. Do you like *me*?"

Michael looked at him: his quick, unflinching black eyes and the enlarged pores round his nose, each with an unctuous droplet emerging from it; an oil and garlic man, quick and fierce, probably also addicted to wine and chili peppers.

"I don't know you…"

"Ah, you know me well enough."

"In that case yes. I suppose I sort of like you; I don't know why."

"Good, that's step one. Now you have to let go of the things you learned in Sardinia. Rome makes good use of this disgusting Mama woman. I ought to do something about her. I think I will, you know."

"A bit of rat poison in her tanks would sort her out," said Michael, wincing with a sudden stab of pain as the words came out of his mouth.

With a frown Giacomo nodded at the overhead monitors, on which they could see groups of armed men purposefully searching the room.

"I wonder what's going through their minds?" said Michael.

"Oh not much, just another day at work. They're looking forward to clocking off for the day, going home, having sausages and chips. They weren't sent primarily to kill you, of course. I was the real target, although it wouldn't have made much difference to you—you weren't supposed to walk out of here, either. I think we'd better get out in case they find the door." Giacomo yawned. "Have you eaten? I'm starving."

"I haven't. We have to pick up a hooker I found in Barcelona. I like her very much. She's waiting for me here in Ripoll."

"That's fine," said Giacomo. "We can pick her up on the way…"

Giacomo

26.

Next morning, Michael woke to the sound of eggs frying.

He could see Paolo, the monk he met yesterday, at the stove deftly manipulating strips of lard and cracking eggs into a black cast-iron pan of impressive size, where already mushrooms and tomatoes were sizzling.

Paolo was wearing baggy underpants and flip-flops. Giacomo was smoking distractedly, waiting for his breakfast and looking out of the window.

Michael yawned as he walked into the kitchen: "Where's Honey?"

"We locked her up. She tried to leave," said Paolo. "I gave her the rest of the heroin. She's more sedate now."

He put a plate in front of Michael, who chewed some of the fibrous lard, then spat it out. "Where do we go now? Where are we, come to think of it?"

"Nowhere special," said Giacomo. "Just a bolt-hole of mine in Barcelona. My public career is over. It doesn't matter; I was tired of the whole thing. Hamming it up for the masses."

He threw a copy of *La Vanguardia* on the table. There was a photograph of him in full regalia, and a caption underneath: "*Ripoll Abbot in Drugs and Prostitution Scandal.*"

"My escape must have annoyed them intensely. They hate bad publicity. Let's face it, they've had enough of it, thanks to all those robed pedophiles." He shook his head: "They did the obvious thing. They capitalized on the fact that I'd abandoned my duties and then the Press Department sprayed some other shit on me. Apparently I've been cavorting with prostitutes; how scandalous is that! I'm to be excommunicated." He sniggered as he shoveled in another forkful.

"Something you mentioned to me earlier, about Günter. Why did he tell me to go to Janine? And then tip you off?"

"Oh, that's easy," said Paolo. "We hate inquisitors like O'Hara and quislings like Mama Maggot."

"In fact we don't actually hate them," said Giacomo. "We'd just rather they weren't here at all."

"That sounds very much as if you hate them."

"Not at all," said Giacomo. "Extermination and hatred are two very different things. If you hate something you want to keep it alive. Hatred is a sort of fixed affection."

"Günter knew you'd end up in St. Helena with O'Hara, and he knew there was a good chance you'd be sent to assassinate Giacomo. Mama Maggot thinks she's as inscrutable as the deep sea, but as far as we're concerned she's a puddle of piddle."

"But you don't hate Günter, do you? And you don't want to exterminate him?"

Paolo and Giacomo burst into fits of giggles. "Günter, how could anyone hate him!" said Paolo. "A lovely Alsatian fellow with a sincere love of sweetmeats? He used to be a very devout person and for all I know he still is. Even Giacomo likes Günter, don't you Giacomo?"

"Yes, of course, our dear, hairy, clawed friend with his devotion to pretty Ariel." Giacomo's greasy lips opened like a ripe fig. "Michael, until you met me you didn't know a damn about anything."

Michael gave him a weary stare. "Until I met you I knew what I was doing. I was putting a bullet in your head. What are you? Just some guy who spouts Latin and eats too much?"

"'*Vos qui peccata hominum comeditis, nisi pro eis lacrimas et oraciones effuderitis, ea que in deliciis comeditis, in tormentis evometis.*'" Giacomo licked his fingers and translated: "'You who feast upon men's sins—unless you pour out tears and prayers for them, you will vomit forth in torment what you eat with pleasure.' I have never been one to feast on sin; I just happen to prefer meat and bread." Giacomo refilled his coffee cup and produced a small, leather-bound book from his dressing gown pocket. It was a selection from C.M Doughty's *Arabia Deserta*. "Do you know, one of the problems of humankind is that we're no longer masters of language and thus we find it almost impossible to understand ourselves? We fight over semantics; we're stuck with clichés and bagatelles. This makes us gross; we can't express who we are anymore. So Michael, if you forgive me I'm going to keep spouting my Latin; I'm a man of words and this is the only way we're ever going to understand anything. Through words." He opened the book with relish. "Listen to this: 'A party of Turcomans have arrived, whose women wear tall red headdresses hung with cornelian-studded plaques of silver gilt...'" He shook his head. "Paolo, what's a cornelian-studded plaque?"

"How would I know?"

"See. And how about this." His stumpy fingers creased the pages in his eagerness: "'...a medley of little houses... some of stone ravished from the monuments.' Notice his use of the word *ravished*, that's true genius."

From the back of the apartment came a sound of insistent hammering. Honey was banging the door, shrieking like a banshee.

"Poor mite," said Paolo. "She's coming into flower and she doesn't know what's happening to her." He looked at Michael. "You might have told her, you miserable fleshpot."

"She would have died if I hadn't stepped in," said Michael.

"Oh, what difference does it make? There's too much talk of *life* these days." Paolo wagged his finger. "A sea urchin has *life*, an amoeba in the ocean has *life*. Life is holy, there's no doubt about that, but we need more focus on *soul*." He attacked his chitterlings with gusto, the impact of his muscular Vulcanic arms rattling the table, then continued: "This poor woman has misplaced her soul. As soon as she's fully transformed we'll have to teach her to fish for it."

"Let's bring her along," said Giacomo. "She seems a pleasant enough kid; I can get her a job as a costume girl at St. Peter's. That's settled, then. Now, Michael, you're probably not aware of the fact that 'Azerbaijan is a dun sweeping country like Spain in winter.' I am, you see, and that's because I spend at least an hour a day reading books that edify the mind... Paolo, what's *rogand*?"

"Shut up, idiot. How should I bloody know?" said Paolo, his face turning livid.

"Shut up? Not very educated, are you, talking like that? *Rogand*, I'll have you know, is a very nice rancid butter eaten in northern Persia."

Paolo thumped down his fist so the glasses jumped. "Giacomo. Can you put that book away and help me make a decision."

"Oh, what? You know perfectly well that we have to go back to Rome and flick O'Hara's nose rather hard. But we're certainly not going anywhere until after breakfast, maybe even after lunch... and I'm going to insist that we're driven there in a decent car with air conditioning. And until we leave," he said petulantly, "I'm going to read my book."

"Rome?" Michael ventured. "What's in Rome?"

"The question is," Giacomo pointed out, "what's not in Rome?" Then continued: "'A covert of poplars'—brilliant use of *covert*. Really sums it up, makes one..."

"So... Rome, then," Paolo interrupted as he rose to his feet. "I shall go and pack and it will take me exactly five minutes, because I own nothing." He walked off, whistling.

"How are you going to flick O'Hara on the nose?" said Michael. "He didn't seem very 'flickable' to me."

"Using my thumb and my index finger." He held up his hand and made a clicking sound. "Like this."

"But you're not going to kill him, are you? Or ask me to kill him?"

"Oh, what a concept." Giacomo guffawed. "You can't kill people, you know; you can only transform them."

"Rome? So you have somewhere we can stay there?"

"Listen: '...roused by the muezzin's unearthly treble... the clamor of vendors and the clatter of hooves will soon begin.'" Giacomo closed the book and continued, with unmistakable finality, like a French blind coming down for the night. "Yes, I have somewhere to stay. Rome is my only true home on earth and has been for about twelve hundred years."

Michael found Honey in a fetal position on the floor, scrabbling about in a pool of blood. "Where were you?" she whispered, lifting her head. "I don't know what's going on. I feel weird. I've had a fucking stomachache since yesterday and really heavy bleeding—which is weird 'cause I had a hysterectomy last year."

"Why don't you have a little talk with Paolo; he'll fill you in," said Michael. "Paolo is a real priest, not like me. He knows all about it."

She eyed him fiercely. "Something's going on and you're not telling me."

"I don't quite know myself. I'm too ashamed to tell you," said Michael. "And anyway you'd never believe me if I told you the truth."

"Yeah, right!" said Honey. "That's what every liar says."

27.

As ever, Rome was luxuriating in the velvety folds of its history. Past midnight, their tinted-glass limousine dropped them at the edge of an enormous plaza, empty but for lunar shadows cast by the columns. In the background lay the floodlit bulk of St. Peter's, a huge illusory shape set against the sky.

Giacomo stretched his back. "Ah, how good to be home." He genuflected towards the dome, without any excessive show of emotion.

Paolo, on the other hand, grabbed his rosary and, with mumbled incantations, fell to his knees.

Honey would not leave Michael's side; she was due to come into full flower that day. He sensed her tremulous presence just behind him, then her hoarse voice whispering into his ear: "Where the fuck are we going? What is this place?"

"St. Peter's. Heard of it?"

"Not really. Some church. Who gives a shit?"

Giacomo interceded, slipping his arm under her elbow and leading her on at a brisk pace. "Come child. Time to disseminate."

As they marched into deep shadow on the west side of the façade they saw men in dark suits and ear-mussels standing by the entrance to the crypts. Respectfully they got out of the way as Giacomo walked confidently towards them, brushing aside a dawdler on the stairs. Once inside, Giacomo and Paolo headed for the wardrobe, where they left their coats and trousers with a girl who gave them ceremonial robes.

"I thought you'd been excommunicated," said Michael.

"Up there I have but not down here," said Giacomo. "Our existence would be too disturbing for the world so we keep it to ourselves. We're very considerate people." He looked at the wardrobe girl and said, with a nod in Michael's direction: "I'd say he needs an alb and a black stole, wouldn't you? With some nice decoration… Ah yes, that one with the fish will be just fine, thank you, my dear."

"What do you do down here? Worship golden calves or something?" said Michael, nervously putting on his robes as he jogged along behind him.

"For now, just be aware of this: '*Ecce ipsi idiote rapiunt celum ubi nos sapientes in inferno mergimur.* The unlearned themselves take heaven by force, while we wise ones are drowned in hell.' St. Augustine, in case you were wondering."

"Don't I get some clothes as well?" moaned Honey.

Paolo, to keep her quiet, gave her a white cotton gown.

They entered a candlelit vault, whose groaning pillars bore the full weight of the Basilica above them. There must have been a thousand people in the dim subterranean chapel. Their silence seemed to take the oxygen out of the air.

The priest and his acolyte stood with their backs to the congregation; busily, they sprinkled holy water on the altar, accessed via a small bridge across a cistern of black undulating water reaching from one transept to the other.

An unseen choir filled the air with wailing dirges. Not pleasant at all, thought Michael. As they were seated in the front pew, he noticed O'Hara at the back inside an island of men in purple robes. He stared bleakly at them across a sea of heads.

The situation was already disturbing enough. But when Giacomo and O'Hara bowed respectfully to each other, it grew stranger still. "What are they doing?" Michael whispered to Paolo, who elbowed him jocularly and said:

"Down here, we try not to be trivial."

"That man tried to kill us, and he'll probably try again."

"So what?" said Paolo. "In killing us he would have been doing us a favor. Anyway, we would have come back another day."

"Some of us don't believe in all that."

"Some of us are about to have their illusions shattered."

Honey pressed herself against him as hypnotic singing rose up from the cistern at the other end. "I've never seen a fucking church like this before. It's like a nightmare; like a goddamn Tom Cruise movie."

A ceremonial golden barge came gliding in. Seven maidens in white tunics stood singing in it, holding out their hands imploringly towards the congregation, then lifting their tunics and revealing their dark, triangular pudenda.

"What are they doing?" Michael whispered to Paolo.

"Praying for fertility, which shall be denied the little slaves."

"So give them rubbers and they'll be fine," said Honey with a smirk.

The doors flew open at the back. A procession of singing children with candles in their hands moved slowly through the congregation, lighting up the gnarled faces of clerics and cardinals.

"They are the blessed ones," Paolo explained. "They were never born."

Again Honey disagreed. "Sorry, father, but they look born enough to me."

The procession stopped when it reached the altar.

The barge began to pull away, while the women on it dropped to their knees, wrung their hands and pulled their hair. They called out to the singing children standing on the footbridge as their craft passed beneath and then glided out of view. The children fell silent and blew out their candles. Darkness fell over the subterranean church, offset by a single candle of massive girth, still burning on its pedestal in the middle of the altar.

Then, with ritual wails, the children filed out.

The congregation was left hovering in a sort of thunderous silence, before the heavy artillery, a group of robed men behind the sanctuary broke into sonorous song to mark the end of the ceremony.

Giacomo stood up and said briskly to Michael. "Would you like a tour before we go home?"

"Okay, why not."

Leaving Honey and Father Paolo behind, Michael followed Giacomo into the atrium, where the worthies had gathered for conversation while wine and cakes were brought round. Unfortunately, O'Hara was waiting for them. Tall and dignified, intent on a bit of explication, he marched forward as soon as he clapped eyes on them.

"Giacomo, dear soul, will you forgive me," he effused, offering his clammy hand. "I was lost; the Devil took me. If anyone knows the ways of the world, its pitfalls and traps, it must surely be you?"

The two men faced each other, each with a sort of hovering moral scrutiny imprinted on his face.

"So go with God, my brother," said Giacomo ceremoniously, "and do not heed the Devil again."

O'Hara frowned. "Yet the Devil tells me I must have you in the vaults where I can venerate your memory—here in the World you stand in my way, my friend." O'Hara threw Michael a sour glance. "And I confess I am dismayed to see this instrument of mine in your hands. His face reminds me of my own transgression."

"I'll keep him, then," Giacomo rejoined, with a glint of mischief. "As a reminder of your moral failings."

Michael found himself grabbed by the scruff of his neck and marched out by Giacomo, whose face, by now, had turned scarlet.

"What's going on?" Michael whispered.

"Bloody hypocrites. Using Satan as an excuse. They are not worthy of their robes or their beards."

"What are those vaults he was talking about?"

Giacomo stopped and recomposed himself. "Ah, yes, the vaults. There's no reason why you shouldn't see them; I think you're ready." He pushed open a side door and they went through a warren of changing rooms and properties stores—Michael saw rows of costumes on rails, pikestaffs and weapons of all descriptions, a wire net filled with stuffed swans; even, vaguely glimpsed as they passed, a cage of monkeys, one of them a noble old orangutan staring forlornly at a twig, as if longing for its home, far away.

The virgins who had earlier exposed themselves and performed the ritual wailing, were now idly chattering, mere actresses removing their makeup in the dressing room.

Giacomo stuck his head in.

"Good work, girls. Excellent performances! You really caught the essence."

"Thanks, Giaconino! Are you coming out with us tonight? We're off to have clam spaghetti."

"It's the ceremony, girls; it's sharpened your appetites. You've asked for fertility and now you're going to hit the town. Your young human bodies are alive to the joys of temptation."

"The old bugger's jealous."

"Poor old sod, he could probably do with a length of *butifarra* himself."

Giacomo smiled. "Bless you," he said. "Been there, done that and bought the cassock."

Decked out in jeans, stiletto heels, and clutch handbags, the girls peered with interest at Michael:

"What about this one?"

"Are you hungry, sweetie? You don't want to spend the night with this old stiff, do you? Come out with us."

Michael twisted uneasily. "Sorry, I don't have time."

Everyone, Giacomo included, seemed to find his answer hilarious. The girls fell about the place laughing, then carefully mopped their tears to avoid smudging their makeup.

Once again Michael felt Giacomo's proprietary hand clutching the back of his neck. "Good Lord. Is that the time? We can't stay here all night." They moved off through peals of renewed laughter, this time down a long corridor with fewer people in it, just a lot of security personnel.

"What was all that about?" said Michael. "I don't get you people. I don't get your jokes."

"That's because you're never been reincarnated."

"And you have?"

"Many, many times, young fellow. Ah, where to begin? I've passed through the ages like a stick in a river."

Michael sighed despondently. "I'm tired. I wish I could just go home."

"And where would that be? Whether you like it or not, Michael, we are your home now. I am your home."

"The fact remains that I don't have a clue what this place is."

"When the top brass decided to commercialize public religion, they thought it would be smart to abolish reincarnation. That was at the Whitby Synod about twelve hundred years ago. We argued all night but there was no stopping them."

"You sound as if you were there."

"In fact I was there, Michael."

"Twelve hundred years ago?"

"Indeed."

"You must have tough maggots to hang around that long. I suppose you have them changed once a month?"

"Oh, certainly. But the human mind gets tired of life; it needs rest. And for this reason we put ourselves into storage from time to time."

He showed an identity card to some guards, who scanned it in an electronic card reader then nodded them through. Heavy steel doors rolled open on thick wheels set into runners in the stone floor. Inside, the air was cool and they seemed to be in a warehouse of sorts. A couple of forklift trucks stood neatly parked along a wall. Shelving units loaded with coffins rose ten meters into the air. At the base of each stack was a list of occupants. "So," said Giacomo, checking a clipboard hanging by a string from a metal strut, "here we have the remains of St. Elizabeth of Hungary, a sweet soul filled with pity for the unfortunates of this world. And here lies St. Benedict, one of our Great Ones. Really he should not be here; he belongs further down."

"Further down?"

"Yes. These depositories go very deep. Even I don't know how many levels there are. You, of course, do not understand why all these dead people are here. You don't comprehend that they're actually alive. Right now they are nothing but shriveled heads with their empty bodies rolled up beneath them and a small film of regularly replenished maggots supplying them with just enough oxygen and nurture to keep the brain alive. Dormant but alive, ready to be brought back at a moment's notice."

He looked at Michael and let this sink in. "Historically speaking, maggothood was conferred on holy people as a reward. Reincarnation was no myth; it was a reality. But somehow the Holy Grail slipped out of our hands. The maggot found a way of escaping the clutches of the Vatican. Slowly, maggot people started popping up all over the place. In 1917, at a closed session of the Vatican Council, they set up an extermination unit. But even today after it's been beefed up a good deal, it rarely manages more than three thousand kills per year. The maggot was our holiest device, our timekeeper and guardian. Even Jesus lies below, in a sacred vault, with His Apostles all round him. But He sleeps very deeply. At various times there have been attempts to resuscitate Him, all unsuccessful." He frowned, peering at Michael as if unsure whether to go on. "There's a war up here between us, Michael, as you have seen. The Pope will not risk a Second Coming of Jesus; he fears it would fail. And the women who enter His chamber to anoint Our Lord and sing for Him inform us that He is far, far away. They say He wouldn't wake even if we found a way of refilling Him. O'Hara, as you have guessed, is a hardliner. He claims that we disrupt spiritual reality. Many times he has refused to take the maggot and join us. He insists he'll meet his Maker in the Kingdom to come. He insists on a real death; he's set on Styx, the fool. Even worse, he's put together a powerful group with some influence in Vatican circles. In my humble opinion, heaven as a concept is a risky strategy. I am not the first to make this assertion, of course; I have been in this flawed world of ours for a long, long time. I am not about to leave it permanently for the sake of a misguided whim."

For the first time Michael realized that there had always been something melancholic about Giacomo's forced hilarity. He patted the older man on the shoulder.

"Maybe there's also something good about the human race? Some tiny aspect?"

Giacomo peered at him with a dubious, pouting mouth. He leaned forward, his face furrowing with intensity. "Dream on, little brother, but do listen to me; I have more experience than you will ever have. Love is a temporary action, and you will learn this if you endure over time as I have. The emotion, however, lasts forever."

"So what this means is that Ariel is still alive? Lying in a box somewhere, because you decided it had to be that way?"

"All things that have been alive are still alive and will always be alive," Giacomo muttered, failing to hide his irritation. "Must you always speak of this wearisome little woman who would have plotted a false trail for you? I on the other hand have mapped out a spiritual path for you. Bear that in mind." His black eyes grew resentful. "Or perhaps my interest in your well-being means little to you?"

Michael staunchly kept to his course. "But when is she coming back?"

"I couldn't possibly answer, my dear fellow. Not without speaking to one of the clerks, and they're not obliged to answer personal enquiries of that kind. She'll be due for reactivation, but not for another couple of hundred years. What difference does it make, anyway? You'll run into her sooner or later. And by the time you do, you won't be the same as you are today."

"I'd rather not wait."

"Who cares what you want?" cried Giacomo. "Who are you? Do you understand how privileged you are to be with me at all?"

"You're only keeping me here to taunt O'Hara and show him you outsmarted him," said Michael, stubborn as ever.

"In fact that is not quite right. I would actually like you to…" He stopped. "I think you know what I'd like you to do."

"Shoot him?"

"Return the favor, let's say."

"I didn't want to be O'Hara's instrument and not yours, either. I want to be my own person."

Giacomo chuckled. "Goodness me, you've been saturated in twenty-first century Western political mythology. You are a pile of organic tissue animated by a life force that comes from God. Humans will always be parasitic on God, Michael, and they will tell you an awful lot of lies as they set about demolishing this planet of ours, for the sake of their mimetic creation of filth."

"Wow," said Michael. "You don't think much of us, do you?"

Giacomo took a deep breath, trying to cool himself; then changed the subject. "I am entrusted with all this, everything you see here. But even I can't just throw sleepers into the tank at the drop of a hat. Everything has to be done with proper regard for ceremony and the blessing of the Council." Then his voice dropped, and with a gentle movement he gripped Michael's shoulder. "Don't worry, my son. Time slips by very quickly once you're oblivious."

Michael closed his eyes. Patience, he told himself. Patience is the only way here. Slowly I will burrow my way into them and begin to understand them. In the mean time I will appeal to them, I will reflect their desires and motivations.

"Let's eat, Giacomo."

The abbot brightened. "That's better, young Michael. Your cleverness is most appealing; your reflective, adaptive personality. You don't fool me for a moment, but ambition has always struck me as a good thing, as long as it does not only tend towards self-importance. I have no self-importance, you see. If I could choose freely, I should like to be alone, far away, in some small, inconsequential town where I had no friends and no duties, and I'd sit on the balcony in the mornings, reading books and minding my own business and never going to church." He smiled fondly. "Although obviously I'd bring Paolo to cook my breakfast and provide a convenient target for irritability. Really, I think that man has been a better companion than any wife could ever have managed; pity he's so inordinately fat or I might have married him."

"I am not ambitious," said Michael. "But I do have desires for my life… which is quite different."

"You're a bit of a spin doctor," said Giacomo. "Even this is a good thing, it is very much the spirit of the age to be a relativist and not have any firm views on anything. I really do think I'll keep hold of you. But first you have to help me clear up this O'Hara nonsense. You're the perfect choice; you're the boomerang."

"The boomerang that hits its target does not come back. If you want to keep hold of me, I know a better way to deal with O'Hara," said Michael with a sinking feeling, which he later identified as guilt. "We can use Honey. It'll be like bread and butter to her."

28.

An hour later, having picked up Paolo and Honey from the empty chapel, they were sitting in Giacomo's ample kitchen in the Vatican City, where Paolo had again stripped down to his underwear to keep his robes from staining, and was frying half a bucketful of small green crabs in oil, tomato, and garlic while a great vat of pasta steamed beside him.

Honey was in a bad mood, confessing to a sudden horniness greater than anything she had ever known. "I can't sleep," she complained, "without visualizing a bulging cock coming towards me. I used to *hate* cocks, you know. I was sick of the sight of them, ugly things with little leery mouths looking at you and always standing to attention like fucking troopers. But now all this has happened to me I almost feel like going back to Barcelona. Except I reckon you're going to tell me I can't do it now I'm a maggot?"

"Stay here a while," said Michael, with a meaningful look at Giacomo. "There are things you could do here for us. You could make a lot of money for yourself, too, enough to buy yourself a little flat."

Paolo slammed the pasta saucepan down on the table. "First she eats," he said irritably, turning to Honey. "And remember, if you do go out to find yourself a man, he must be brought back here for safekeeping in the cellar until he flowers. And then we have to take proper care of him. We're not animals!" He brought

out a large pasta fork and started ladling out gargantuan por-
tions, while at the same time gently shaking Honey by the arm.
"And then you have to be chaste after that, fill yourself with drugs
and drink, or just eat enormous quantities of food as we do. Of
course you must also spend a great deal of time in prayer. I will
teach you the prayers."

"Save it, father; sounds like a bore to me," said Honey, her
mouth full of oil-soaked bread. "The only priest I ever liked was
Father Tuck, you know him? I hate these goddamn maggots, and
I hate you, Michael, for infecting me in the first place."

"Infecting, that's a big word!" said Michael. "You were like
a skeleton when I saw you; frankly, you were already diseased—
that's one of the reasons I chose you. A good maggot always se-
lects his targets, you know. Now you have hundreds of years of
life ahead of you; is that so bad?"

"Or a few weeks, depending on how you behave yourself,"
Giacomo added laconically.

"So what? At least I was enjoying myself." She pointed a
bony finger at Michael. "You took everything from me; I can't
even take a decent shit any more. I just sit there while a couple
of pellets come out of my ass. Who wants to knock around for
hundreds of fucking years, anyway? What you supposed to do
with yourself, play poker all day or take up knitting?"

"Why all this negativity?" Giacomo threw in. "I have known
maggots who get interested in gambling or horse racing and find
that it keeps them busy and satisfied for centuries. Or money-
making, that's a very good one. If you take out a really good
investment plan and bribe one of the people downstairs to book
you in for rebirthing in fifty years, you'll be awake before you
know it and then you cash in your bonds and go on holiday.
How's that?"

"I'd rather be a corpse, and so would you lot if you weren't
such pussies."

There was some truth in what she said.

Awkwardly they changed the subject.

Giacomo stuck his finger into the sugo and tasted it, then gulped a mouthful of his beloved Piedmonte wine before Paolo jostled him away from his stove. "In fact, my dear girl, this gives me an excellent idea. You are very fresh and your host is feeling very boisterous right now. You need to cleave to its requirements."

"Put that in plain fucking English, will you!"

"I'd be glad to. You have to do what they want or they'll eat you alive. Right now they want to swarm. You can either choose to go and find yourself a sad rover and bag him; or, if you're more enterprising, track down a fallen cleric who shouldn't be screwing in the first place."

"Yeah, I know what you're talking about. Michael told me all about O'Hara, I even saw him; he's a seedy little swine."

"I didn't know you'd been briefed." Giacomo's eyes flickered in Michael's general direction. "Thanks, dear boy."

"Is it because I'm a hooker?" said Honey. "You think hookers don't understand things? We're quick as lightning, if you want to know. And we have a fucking state-of-the-art asshole alarm and right now it's ringing in here, very loud." She tapped the side of her head. "By the way this crab tastes like shit."

Giacomo watched her mawkishly, but again chose to ignore her outburst. "Cardinal O'Hara says his murderous instincts aren't his fault. He says it's the Devil making him do it."

"I've met types who talk like that and usually they just came out of the nuthouse." Honey screwed up her face, processing the information. "So why does O'Hara hate you so much? And you know what? I don't get why the Pope gives money to maggot people and lets 'em live under his church and at the same time has 'em killed by the score. I can't get my fucking head round it."

Giacomo nodded confidently. "I think I can answer that one. The Hydra is a dangerous monster because she suffers from a multiple personality. She'll kiss you with one head, but with her other heads she'll petrify, savage, poison, nibble, spit or mutter evil curses at you."

"It's not that," said Paolo. "It's because the Catholics fear us. It's the fear of the Other."

"The other fucking *what*?" said Honey.

Giacomo sighed. "Maggot people can't have children. Which means there'll be fewer people around, which means a lot of empty churches and less money and a heck of a lot of Catholic priests out of a job. The Church doesn't like that, of course; it doesn't like maggots getting too numerous."

Honey nodded. "Well, people do have to work, you know. Or they starve. O'Hara's making sense if that's what he's about."

"Never mind about him making sense. He's an old anaconda and we'd like you to seduce him," said Giacomo. "Maggotize him for us, would you dear? So we can keep him lingering with us for hundreds of years and torment the heck out of him."

"So that's all I get? A dry old fucker like O'Hara who smells like he forgot to change his underwear for a month? You know what? If I could live without men like him I would, but it looks like I'm stuck with them. If I do it anyway, if I do it for your sake, what will you do for me?"

"Well, you won't be needing any other men at all, that's for sure," Paolo cut in. "That's what we'll do for you; we'll free you from their pernicious influence. Afterwards you could go to Mama Maggot in Sardinia; she might even take you on as a lay sister."

Giacomo agreed. "Yes indeed. Then all you do is lie about and occasionally make a little excursion to the city to pick up maggot fodder. It's an easy life; you stay on a cushion all day, eat piglets in the evening, take a few hits and watch the sunset over the sea." He frowned at Paolo and spoke under his breath: "Or are we missing an opportunity? Should we give her a gun and ask her to kill the old bitch for us?"

Michael stepped in. "If you send Honey to St. Helena she'll be the one who ends up dead. They'll find out who she is and what she's done and they won't even have to kill her; they'll just deny her when she's due."

"Keep your worries to yourself!" Giacomo shot him a poisonous glance. But when he refocused on Honey he was unctuous: "Whatever you want, my dear girl, we can make it happen for you. We have enormous reserves of money, we have a portfolio of quite beautiful properties all over the world, and we have an endless supply of drugs and fresh maggot. How about an island off the coast of Thailand? Or a penthouse in Tokyo? Just rid us of this Cardinal and it can all be yours. We'll open the coffers for you; you can take what you want."

"You don't have to go for the hard sell. I'll do it just because I'm bored stiff and I fancy a challenge," she said.

"First we have to tell you how to snare him. We know all about his appetites," said Paolo.

"Yeah, yeah! You're going to teach me how to get some twisted old geezer's rocks off. You rate yourselves, don't you?" She shook her head in wonder. "Just give me his fucking address, I'll stake out his place tonight. And if I don't see him I'll go back tomorrow."

"Take care, he's not a nice man," said Michael.

"Don't you worry, mister, I always did take care of myself. I met a lot of bad men and I was fine until the day I met you."

29.

"I am grateful to you, Michael," said Giacomo, after Honey, loudly complaining, had been taken off to a nunnery. "I've rarely felt so murderous, but you are quite right; it is much prettier to let O'Hara choose his own gin-trap. Messier, too." He chuckled contentedly.

They were standing on a palace roof inside the Vatican compound, looking out over the myriad housetops and television aerials of Rome.

"It all seems so violent," said Michael.

"Ah, you think so?" The old man shook his head with wonder. "I've seen so much death and violence over the years, I no longer think of humans as anything but deranged, thoroughly objectionable, psychopathic apes. I'd prefer them all dead and buried in mass graves."

Michael shuddered. Giacomo's humanity had withered like a fruit left too long in the sun. He'd been tempered and shriveled, salted and oiled, until finally he lay potted under a screw-top lid and bore no resemblance to his original nature. Yet, in spite of this, some tiny portion of it remained as a super-concentrated essence, and this was the charming part.

"Are you wondering why I've brought you up here? Did you think it was just to admire the view?"

Michael decided to be truthful. "No. I suspect you have some reason, and I am hoping I won't be threatened or arm-twisted or in some other way turned against myself."

"How unfair you are! How spoiled and self-pitying. I treat you almost like my son. I agonize over your spiritual development."

"I'd rather just be left in peace."

"Left in peace. Ha! Who wouldn't?" Giacomo's hand made a sweeping motion, taking in the entire city. "Flawed," he said. "All flawed. Give up your hopes, abandon your illusions, they are not serving you." As he turned to look at his young protégé, Giacomo's eyes had a strange light in them, a mixture of guilt, eagerness, and affection, emotions that seemed left over in his psyche like driftwood washed up. "I tell you this now because I need you to understand."

"Understand what?"

"Why, yourself. What else is there to understand?"

"I feel I've done everything you could possibly ask. Now I want to have some freedom. And I'd like to understand why Ariel had to be taken from me. Why couldn't you let us be together? I love her, you know..."

"Ariel! Good Lord, the fuss you make about her. And as for freedom..." His face softened. "But you are young, I was also young once. The problem with wanting a thing, Michael, is that it almost always takes you away from your true needs. It would be better for humans not to want so much; they're not equipped for their own ambitions and they won't pay for their desires. Humans want a free lunch and there's no such thing; any quantity surveyor could tell you that."

From downstairs, in one of the expansive salons, came the voices of a hundred diners, the slamming of their cutlery, loud voices declaiming. While in Rome, Giacomo and Paolo felt it was good politics to have the inner circle over for dinner two or three times per week—for feasting and scheming.

Michael hung on. "I'm not an opportunist. I do want to survive, though, and I'd like to *enjoy* surviving."

"You're very fond of making irrelevant distinctions. But I forgive you, I forgive you as a man who once held a gun to my head and chose freely not to shoot. But yes… survival… this bugbear of our race, a remnant from our time in caves." Giacomo laughed bitterly. "Look at this vast city filled with lost sheep struggling to survive. They think they need money, preferment. They'll grasp at anything; they're drowning in ignorance."

There was a scrape of a metal door behind them, and when they looked round, they saw Paolo stooping as he emerged. "Thank goodness, you're still here," he said. "I thought you might have…"

"Might have what?" said Giacomo ferociously, as if afraid that Paolo was going to say too much. "I am having a quiet word with Michael, if you please."

"Ah…" Paolo stopped indecisively in the doorway. "Should I go?" When Giacomo failed to answer, the monk simply held out his hand and muttered a quiet blessing in Michael's direction: "'*Amici, ascende superius*,' that is all you need to know for now. 'Ascend higher, my friend'. For in the bone house none will be able to recognize your bones. You'll be dead and gone."

"Why are you telling me all these things?" said Michael. "Are you going away?"

Paolo and Giacomo grew shifty. Their thoughts seemed to rise up, whirling about and skimming across the flushed evening sky like starlings hesitant to settle for the night.

Then Paolo said: "Yes, we are going away."

"And you can no longer go through life as a stupid little prick from Provence who wants his girlfriend back," said Giacomo. "You have to give her up."

The two men inched towards the door. "We'll take our leave, then," said Giacomo, with a little wave. "God-speed."

Paolo came forward and offered his hand for Michael to kiss, which he did, reluctantly: it stank of garlic and vinegar.

"Don't let me down," said Giacomo in the background. "Don't sadden me."

"I don't think you could be saddened by anyone."

Paolo intervened again: "An ambitious man does not have time for sadness, and that is because his time is valuable and he has many things to do before he sleeps."

30.

Cardinal Patrick O'Hara reclined in his favorite chair by the fire, sipping a cup of first-flush Darjeeling while he waited for the Mercedes Pullman to turn up. He was on his way to a private service at St. Stephen's Chapel of the Abyssinians, far from the unwelcome crowds and their beloved cameras.

In another age, long ago, congregations had watched services through carved screens—had not even understood the chants and rituals, which were all in a different language from their own. Religion had been a mystery in those days. People had done as they were told and the priesthood held sway over society.

But democracy had invaded the world and now they were bound by its simplistic rules.

It had been a heavy night for his soul, one in which he had besmirched himself with a harlot. The narrow lane outside was usually deserted, but today he had seen her several times on the corner, a long-legged stork of a woman in a yellow leotard and tiny latex skirt, tottering unsteadily over the cobblestones in her thigh-length boots. Her availability had made him savage and restless. Ritually he'd repeated one of his favorite maxims, from St. Augustine, 'God is to be enjoyed, creatures only used as means to that which is to be enjoyed.' After his long, empty life, why should he not enjoy the delicacies on which others habitually gorged? It was a disturbing and delicious thought. Also a venal sin, yet why so venal? What in the name of God was so venal about reaching out and plucking the sweet cloven fruit of womanhood? Murder, yes, that was certainly an offense to His eyes. Murder had become commonplace—the death squads were constantly liquidating maggots. And most certainly it was justifiable.

He had kept it brief, up against the wall in the vestibule, then paying the jade what she asked—but he knew repentance would be more long-drawn.

He reflected on his long life of struggle, wondering, in spite of all, why he cared so much about people's stuffing—whether of maggot or flesh?—when patently they were all human beings anyway.

Ah, what a life of melancholy. To be so alone! He thought of his old home in Limerick: the house where he was born, a crumbling unpainted smudge littered with a few sticks of worm-eaten furniture. A smell of dust that could not be got rid of, because the place itself was dust. The larder, stocked with dry beans and unmentionable tins containing nothing that could be eaten, unless his mother applied her utilitarian hand, which she only did at regulated times. The poverty of those days still made him shudder when he thought of it. Splintered floorboards without linoleum. Rats breeding behind the skirting boards, crawling wood lice drowned in the sink in the mornings. His father in his lumpy chair, fiddling with the wireless and solemnly listening to the King's speech as if it made any difference to him. Outside, the garden with its tall rustling grass they had no mower to cut.

Only the church bells, ringing out for evensong, had moved his spirit back then. He had given his life to it. The Church, the behemoth, this human invention, an enormous whirlpool sucking more and more into itself, like a glutton at a table.

He shook his head to be rid of the memory; but when he peered out of the window at the dreary dark skies, he found it difficult to believe that there'd be some green, bright valley up there, where he'd be welcomed after his death.

You are a murderer and a wanton, he told himself. Who would welcome you?

Reeling with disquiet, O'Hara went to the great Venetian mirror in the hall and stood there studying his face in the mirror. Every furrow, every wrinkle and every twitch spoke of deep unhappiness; an unsmiling aspect in all that he had ever attempted.

You have acted out the iniquities and vices you always secretly longed for. Nonetheless you must take a stand against them.

I will be their inquisitor; I will fry the very gizzards of their apostasy, until their bones crack with loud splitting sounds and their brains come bubbling out of their miserable skulls, I will spill their churning guts; their pleas for mercy shall be as music to my ears.

Strength seemed to come churning back as these dark words rose up in him:

A day will come when people thank me for keeping the human race pure of this filth, this churning, slithering filth that threatens the very backbone of the human project.

Ah, how fine a phrase that is.

The human project.

A shining city on a hill.

A million willing throats pouring out their hearts in sacred song.

By the time he had sponged himself down, brushed his thinning hair, put on his pressed woolen cape and walked down the winding staircase, the long black car was already waiting outside, its engine idling. He settled into the soft leather back seat with a contented sigh. "St. Stephen's," he muttered to the driver, who did not answer or move. After a long minute, O'Hara leaned forward and repeated in a stern voice: "I said, St. Stephen's!"

When the driver turned round, O'Hara's evening took a decisive turn for the worse. Because the man sitting there in the driver's seat was not his usual. In fact, he'd been replaced by Brother Paolo—the gluttonous maggot-monk.

"Good evening, Cardinal. We're waiting for a few people. If you don't mind."

At that moment, the doors opened on either side. Giacomo climbed in next to O'Hara, and an anonymous non-speaking type in a dark windcheater got in on the opposite side. He didn't show O'Hara he was armed; he didn't have to.

The car accelerated away strongly.

O'Hara was agape for an instant, then quickly found his stride. "What is this? I have a service to attend to, brother Giacomo. I'm expected."

"It'll have to wait," said Giacomo. "We're invited to a dinner party and we thought you'd like to come. You seem so damned miserable all the time. If you were a dog I'd throw a bucket of water over you, give you a good wash, then a pile of marrowbones. And that's precisely what I'm going to do—even though you're not a dog."

"Although you could be if you want to," added Paolo from the front.

O'Hara leaned back, puzzled. "Do you not hear I'm expected somewhere?"

"Expected, yes. Certainly expected. But unfortunately, owing to unforeseen circumstances…" said Paolo, without taking his eyes off the road.

"The point is, my brother," said Giacomo, "You sipped from the sacred well tonight. In ten days or so you'll be bursting into leaf, if you see what I mean."

Paolo slowed down the great car and picked up Honey on a street corner.

She got in with a guffawing laugh. "You again," she said, peering at him. "But I'd know you better if you dropped your pants."

O'Hara felt his mind spinning and, in the same instant, grew aware of an insistent slithering feeling inside his urethra.

Oh, fucking maledictions!

He tried to speak, but his tongue seemed to have recoiled into the back of his throat. The calamity had come. The locusts were swarming over his pastures. His house was burning. There was also an unexpected feeling, which he analyzed many times after. It was relief. Everything was lost. No longer would he have to carry all that luggage, all those boxes and crates and packages.

No more burdens.

From now on I shall please myself, he thought, looking at Honey and imagining what else he'd inflict on her, next time.

These thoughts were intensely private, of course. To the others in the car O'Hara presented the very picture of a man in the grip of remorse and regret—groaning, wailing, oozing with self-castigation.

Only Honey showed any empathy at all. She turned round and subjected him to a lengthy examination, then said: "If I were you, which thank fuck I'm not, I'd let yourself go a bit. No one minds a guy who likes to get his end away. Most women like it; why don't you look at it that way? What could be worse than ending up with some bloke who just sits there and reads the frigging newspaper?"

Giacomo hooted with laughter, but Honey silenced him with a glare.

"Very well put," said Giacomo. "I could transpose what you just said into better language and it would be a perfectly well argued piece of…"

"Yeah, well, I'm not like you. I speak fucking English."

"Shut up," O'Hara cried. "All of you. I can't listen to this, you're all foul, revolting people without any sense of…"

"I must admit I can appreciate your position," Paolo cut in. "Being a maggot is not for the fainthearted. That's why we thought we'd give you a choice."

Something in Paolo's voice stopped O'Hara short, made him sink into oblivious silence. The choice to do what? Nothing pleasant, to be sure.

His question was about to be answered.

On the outskirts of Rome the car left the autostrada and, after a few winding roads, turned down a bumpy track into a large walled and gated olive grove. In the middle, where the trees thinned, some twenty or thirty people were waiting for them. There were tables, sofas and cushions. Waiters hovered in the background. A log fire had been prepared earlier; the embers lay deep now and were easily hot enough to transform a human body into a skeleton in an hour or two.

They got out of the car. "If you prefer," said Paolo, "this will be your cremation fire. As a special favor to you, if you'd like us to, we'll scatter your ashes over Jerusalem."

"Of course you might prefer to spend the evening here, with us?" Giacomo added. "It's not such a bad night for sitting under the stars. And this is a good fire; really it would be a huge shame to sully it with human fat when we have brought sucking pigs nicely skewered and ready for roasting as well as a barrel of fine Nepente from Sardinia. Why don't we just roast these piglets, drink this wine? We have fruits of the field, figs, peaches, with cream and vanilla—even a couple of harlots for corrupted appetites."

"So the question you're being asked," said Paolo, "is whether you want to enjoy your life? There's no need to follow Giacomo's gluttonous path. Perhaps you'd rather be a good Dualist—stay clear of meat, partake only of fish and avoid sex altogether?"

O'Hara thought about it. Without a doubt, he was tired of earthly light constantly bombarding his optical nerve with its babbling irrelevance. But suicide was certainly not an option. He was not about to give up on his great sacrifice now and, in so doing, assure himself of damnation.

The fierce heat from the fire-pit burned against his skin. He stared down at the churning pool of vermilion, trying to remember if he had any principles left and, if so, what they were.

31.

The following day, Michael seemed to be a prisoner of sorts in a monastery. He had a cell and a hard bed and not much else to occupy him except an abridged copy of Augustine's *City of God*.

Even the food was lackluster. Not so much as a lamb chop or a glass of ale.

As evening set in he lost his patience and went to the door, repeatedly thumping it with all his might until he heard soft footsteps coming down the corridor.

"What ails you, brother?" someone said on the other side of the door.

"What fucking ails me is I don't know why I'm being kept here. Where's Giacomo?"

The answer, when it came, was unexpected.

Some sort of lever was pulled, he heard a screeching sound of pulleys and wheels turning. A large section of the floor beneath him gave way. For a split second he seemed to hover in the air, looking about him and wishing he was lying on the bunk or standing by the window admiring the view or in fact doing anything but hanging there in temporary suspension, nervously peering down a black shaft right under his feet.

Then he began to fall.

At first there was darkness, before he noticed tiny blue lamps sweeping by at dizzying speed.

Slowly the gradient of the shaft changed and he found him-self sliding along a shiny, padded surface at a furious rate of knots. It was difficult to say for how long. It seemed like several minutes, but it must have been much less. Now and then he heard some-one roaring just behind him. He looked round, expecting to see a figure in pursuit of him, until he realized that he was actually making the sound himself, and it was somehow echoing back at him.

An enormous sadness welled up in him. Images of his par-ents appeared. His mother, her cleanness and modesty. How he missed her. Then his father, his darling father, struggling with his demons and finding no damned peace wherever he went in the world. He even saw their house in Borehamwood, his puzzled grandmother in the top room—like a downy chick in a huge bed filled with ripped feather bolsters—and her constant de-mands for chicken soup.

The incline seemed to flatten out. His descent slowed, and he dropped heavily into a deep pile of straw.

He sat up and looked around, finding himself in an odd-shaped metal cage whose bars were like a giant rib cage. There was nothing much in there, just a pitcher of water, a hunk of dry bread, and, in a corner, a bucket. Overhead was an enormous vault, a space hollowed directly into solid rock, decorated all the way to the top with symmetrical florets, everything dimly lit by candles of enormous girth.

The exit doors looked strong enough to withstand a nuclear blast.

He heard a voice: "They always have to screw with your brain, Michael. Just because it's the only thing you have that's actually yours."

He saw something moving in the straw at the other end of the cage. A tousled head of hair appeared, and beneath it, a sleepy face and mischievous eyes.

Ariel!

The first moments passed in astonished recognition. There was a jolt of recognition as he moved closer to her smell, the shape of her arm and the softness of her neck. He pressed his face into her.

"You made it, Ariel. I knew you would."

"I didn't exactly make it. They put me here."

"We're here; that's all that matters."

"You soft git." She stroked his hair, delighted in spite of herself, but also hurried. "I'm sorry but there's very little time. We have to prepare; we'll have time to talk another day. Let go of me, let go of your life, Michael. There's no escape, there's no way out of this and not even an ending. Soon our little friends above will lay on a procession for us with singing and music," she said. "They'll come down here and take us away to the stripping room. Then empty us, hang us up to dry off, roll us up in coffins and leave us for a couple of hundred years. As a special privilege, they said, they'd put us in the same box. Isn't that touching?" When she saw his horrified face, she added: "Don't worry. It sounds a hell of a lot worse than it is. To be honest, I was glad to wake up in Purissima's kitchen sofa. I needed to find you, Michael; I had to talk to you and say sorry. If it hadn't been for that I'd rather have stayed where I was. In the end that's the really sad part about maggot people. They find life such a pain. They can't bring themselves to admit it, but they'd really prefer to be rolled up in a coffin, off and away in their dream worlds. The dutiful ones, like those two fellows you've been knocking about with, try to make some kind of coherent ideology of it all... but the bottom line is they can't wait to get their heads down."

Michael felt a sting of pain at the thought of Giacomo and Paolo, their pleasant banter over many a breakfast. He remembered first setting eyes on Giacomo behind the secret door in the priory. His quick and salty wit had given him vital sustenance. In many ways Michael actually loved Giacomo, also his faithful Paolo.

"You mustn't be taken in by their humanity, Michael; it's only skin deep," said Ariel and gave his hand a little squeeze. "What we have, my darling, is something few others of our kind will ever experience. We love each other; they don't know what that means."

"And that's another reason for putting us into storage?"

"Correct. It's a contributory reason. As far as they're concerned, this is our chance to have a little chat before we're put to sleep. Then once they've polished off the human race, killed off the cities, and mopped up any remaining strays, they'll bring us back. Probably they'll even give us a little pension, enough to take a suite at the Cannes Carlton and drink champagne cocktails for breakfast." Leaning forward, she whispered, "Until the end of time," and placed a puckered kiss on the end of his nose. "So that's the theory. In practice, they forget about you, they always do. The brass plate on your coffin grows dusty; from time to time if you're lucky some archivist gives it a polish and looks up your name in a book and says 'Aha', and you rattle around in the vaults for a few hundred years more and then when your time comes you're chucked in the maggot tank. Before you know it you're standing on your own two legs again, wondering what the hell that was all about." She laughed. "And that's the only good point about these Gnostic bastards. Suddenly the people who salted you away are also decommissioned. A new generation takes over... with a new set of hang-ups. That means you probably won't have to deal with the same *cunts* who gave you a hard time in your last life. Of course you could be unlucky—you could wake up and find the same tossers still running the place."

"Tell you what," he said, "before those candles burn down, let's give them a real surprise. Let's get out of here."

"Funny."

"I did it once before, remember? You told me to do it; you could tell me again."

"Michael, it's time to settle up!" Her green eyes shone with agitation. "You have to understand most maggot people are just slithering sacks with a semi-vegetal brain on top and a gnawing urge to fuck. They couldn't punch their way out of a paper bag, let alone an underground dungeon. You may not like to hear this, but you're going to have to face up to it. You're not so different. And neither am I."

32.

The subterranean Gnostic basilica was filled to bursting with dignitaries watching with outraged disbelief as Cardinal O'Hara, once the most outspoken of all maggot critics, lifted the Holy Grail to his lips and, visibly disgusted, swallowed its squirming contents. The congregation seemed to hold its breath as he struggled against the gagging reflex. The sound of his gulp, with the movement of his Adam's apple, drew wails from the back pews— where his most dedicated supporters had gathered. When the ceremony was over, the top brass retired to the da Vinci Chambers—a room designed to be an exact replica of the artist's *Last Supper* painting, with a long table on a dais at the front. Here sat the replica Apostles, slightly elevated above the lesser ecclesiasts at rough trestle-and-board tables. Bread and wine were served, but it wasn't quite as impoverished as it seemed; the bread was stuffed with beluga or veal. The wine was sublime, transubstantiation in its own right.

Not ten minutes into their supper, O'Hara clattered his jeweled goblet and stood up. "May I humbly ask," he said pompously, "for a few moments of your precious time?" Silence fell in fits and starts. O'Hara looked down on his enemies and bared his teeth in a ferocious, reflective smile. "We all know that in our congregation there has always been a lot of quarrelling between friends. This is inevitable. When people care about things they are always bound to see different solutions… and resolutions…" he blundered.

"Nicely put, Cardinal," someone roared.

There was scattered laughter. Who the heck did this O'Hara shit think he was, coming here and drinking from the Holy Grail and behaving as if he had some sort of authority? O'Hara swallowed hard, looking out over a sea of hostile ecclesiasts nodding and conferring amongst themselves while knocking back huge amounts of red wine. Waiters sprinted round with ten-liter flagons, continuously refilling the carafes on the tables.

My God, he thought. This is not a Christian congregation; this is something diabolical. I must steel myself. He raised his hand and soldiered on. "The quarrel in our beloved Church has always been this: should we make Eden, or should we pray for it. And the answer, my dear friends, is that... I no longer know." He raised his hand. "But I will say this..."

Giacomo stood up abruptly, with a scrape of his heavy chair. "Thank you, Brother O'Hara, for sharing your uncertainties. Now if you wouldn't mind shutting up for a moment."

This time there was a roar of laughter. Then to his right, a bishop from Trieste, in the very action of raising his goblet to his mouth whilst fiercely cackling at Giacomo's retort, was struck instantly dead. His stare grew glassy as he slumped forward and spilt his wine over the table.

So silent was the room that, as the wine dripped onto the flagstone floor, each drop seemed like a spurt of blood from a severed artery.

And yet there was something routine about this death.

A group of waiters came running in. By their combined efforts they had soon removed the dead bishop and even wiped the table where his crumbs now seemed an offense against decency.

Slowly, conversation resumed everywhere; muttered words, small-talk... all trying with every fiber in their beings not to give in to panic.

Giacomo frowned deeply, lingering on the spot where the bishop had sat alive and well not ten minutes ago. In the last month, he had lost three abbots, one bishop, a cardinal and close to twenty priests in Italy alone.

No one liked to say so, but the fact was: mortality was back.

The maggot, once a guarantee of immortality, had become a lottery. Their ranks were being depleted. Maggots were dropping everywhere.

Giacomo turned to Paolo: "O'Hara's finished eating. Why not show him round?"

Paolo wiped his mouth on his sleeve. "Absolutely." Then, turning to O'Hara: "Come on, let's go."

The two clerics set off arm in arm, looking like two friends reminiscing about the good old days.

Two discreet guards accompanied them.

"Don't try anything," said Paolo. "I'll blade-bugger you if so much as *fart* without my say-so."

"So this is it, is it?" O'Hara said, looking at Paolo. "You'll suck my innards out and dump my head in a coffin for five hundred years."

"Well, not yet we won't. You haven't blossomed yet."

"But once I have?"

"What have you really done to deserve the light? There are others competing for the same privilege, most of them far worthier than you. Particularly now that people are actually dying, we have to weigh up who we should keep. And of course we won't keep people who make a nuisance of themselves," said Paolo. "You know what Giacomo's like. He likes a quiet life, so he can concentrate on recipe research and eating."

The two men made their way down a long corridor that reached far into the gloom. O'Hara was doing his best not to look too impressed by the scale of the caverns, which he'd never seen firsthand although of course he'd heard all about them. Instead he took refuge in disapproval. "Who paid for all this?" he said. "It must have swallowed up huge resources over the years."

"Oh, we constructed it all with our own hands, and with faith, of course; nothing can be done without that," said Paolo smugly, although he knew very well how enormous the bills had been since the expansion program.

"So what's next? Are you going to frog-march me to the gutting rooms?"

"I can show them to you," Paolo offered. "We have time. I was going to check on our protégés, Michael and Ariel, but we can do it afterwards. They're undergoing self-purification in readiness for enshrinement."

"You do have some lovely words to describe disgusting things."

33.

Shadowed by two clinking bodyguards, the two men came down a long concrete corridor more or less like an underground military complex, lit by sodium lights.

Brother Paolo was still holding his old enemy firmly by the arm.

"If you'd be kind enough to accompany me this way," he said, eagerly turning off into an ultra-modern passage, the walls of which were decorated with silver fish moving in highly decorative shoals towards a gilded arch lit by shimmering lights, a sort of imitation of sunlight passing through water: "We commissioned this installation; it was done by a Dane. You know, they really are the best at design—of course she had to be maggotized afterwards to keep her quiet." Paolo's grip tightened. "Come on, I'll show you the new processing center. We're very proud of it."

As they entered an expansive, brightly lit complex, O'Hara felt he had entered a world of fiction—an industrialized, genocidal facility of the spirit.

There was a good deal of machinery in there: tracks ran beneath the ceiling, with hooks sliding along, locking onto and picking up tubular aluminum chairs lowered by an automated crane.

A group of naked maggot people on what looked like a train platform were preparing for their imminent retirement. Some were smoking, others embracing or talking emotionally to friends who had come to wave them goodbye from an auditorium to one side. One, probably an Englishman, was calmly leafing through a newspaper while taking long thoughtful swigs from a bottle and puffing on a pipe. Beside him, a woman was undressing and carefully folding her clothes and some other personal effects into a regulation-size case. An orderly behind a counter, having presented her with various documents to sign, attached these to the case and then threw it onto a slow-moving conveyor belt; it passed through a scanning device before exiting through a small gate hung with undulating plastic strips.

"Now watch," said Paolo, as the Englishman folded up his newspaper and left it on a table, then eased himself into a vacant chair like a traveler getting into his seat.

A young priest adjusted his armrests, fixed his head in a clamp, and unceremoniously sprayed his buttocks with a lubricating unction—then joined him in a quick prayer before sending him on his way.

O'Hara stared with mounting horror.

The chair drew level with an industrial robot, which swung into action, inserting its long snout through an opening at the base of the chair into the rear end of the passenger, then made a whining sound. As the machine sucked, the man collapsed like a balloon—only the head was unaffected, held in place by rubberized prongs at the top.

Once extraction was finished—a procedure that took no more than three or four seconds—the robot withdrew its nuzzle. There was another short interval before a green light flashed and an all-clear signal rang out. The machinery jerked into motion again with much clattering of metal.

At the other end of the production line, the chair slid onto a secondary track. Workers in white overalls unceremoniously unhooked the body-skin and transferred it to what can only be described as wheeled clothes-horse.

There was one final stage in the operation. The head was tagged through its left ear with a bar-code, then scanned using a

small handheld device. Once the wheeled units were fully loaded, they were slowly pushed through vats of heavy-duty moistur-
izer, then left in a drying room, from where O'Hara heard the
whirring of giant fans.

"This is monstrous," he whispered, feeling his legs almost
giving way beneath him. "I thought I was beyond forgiveness; I
see now that I am nowhere near as wicked as…"

"We can handle up to about two hundred and forty extrac-
tions per hour," said Paolo, a certain pride and professionalism
in his voice as he watched the system in action. "We got the top
people at Fiat to help us design the process. For now we're focusing more on extraction than refills—we haven't re-modernized
that stage yet, but eventually we'll use that cavern over there for
it." He waved his arm towards a large, uneven opening in the
rock wall at the far end. "The capital outlay is incredibly costly,
so we thought we'd leave it for now. As we won't be doing much
refilling for the next hundred years or so, it wouldn't be prudent
to shell out all that money now. At this stage it's all about safe
storage. We have space for about a million sleepers, and that
should do us for now."

"And you expect me to go through this. To sit on one of
those things and…" O'Hara said.

Paolo gave him a little pat on the arm. "Don't worry, you'll
go through it all right," he said. "We all will. It will be done
hygienically and safely and we'll be brought back when the time
is right. See it as a blessing, if you can. Every person who enters
this room is one of the chosen." He sighed, and threw an envious
look at the people waiting on the platform. "I'll have to wait at
least a hundred years before I can retire… That's a day I'm looking forward to enormously." Then, with a glance at his watch:
"We must press on."

They returned to the corridor—O'Hara still feeling his legs
rather wobbly—and descended a few levels into far gloomier parts
of the catacombs, where dungeons were still dungeons, with all
the usual attributes such as cobwebs, Gothic columns, and oak

doors. They reached the massive doors leading to Michael and Ariel's cell.

"This area will be preserved for its historical value," said Paolo. "I expect one day it'll be a museum of sorts..." He hauled up a sturdy chain fastened in the depths of his pocket, then selected a small key from his burgeoning key ring and opened an electrical cupboard. Inside was a monitor, which he turned on. A high definition black-and-white image showed the cavern within. Using a joystick he rotated the camera, but there was no sign of those within—no sign at all.

With a frown Paolo punched in a code and pressed a large green button. The doors swung open soundlessly. He went inside for a closer look, but it was empty. He stood thunderstruck for a moment.

O'Hara inspected the cave, noting the chute coming out of the wall, the rib-shaped cage and the piles of straw. His mood lifted considerably. "There's nothing lovelier than a prison with broken doors," he called out gleefully. "Makes an old Paddy like me think he's still in with a chance, know what I mean?"

"Shut up, idiot. Let me think."

But there wasn't a great deal of thinking Paolo needed to do. He went back to the electrical cupboard and picked up a telephone.

Giacomo was sitting at his desk, thoughtfully looking at a custard roly-poly he'd been brought by one of the lay sisters— whose family's bakery was famous in Rome for its pastries. The custard had just enough solidity to prevent it from oozing, yet enough lightness to avoid lumpiness.

Beauty walks the razor's edge, thought Giacomo.

At this exact moment, the telephone, that ugly shrill modern invention, made its presence felt. Telephones were harbingers of bad news, disaster, and annoyance. He glared for a good while, then snatched it up and spluttered into the receiver: "Yes! What is it?"

"Michael and Ariel. They've gone," Paolo announced breathlessly at the other end of the line. "I've searched their cell more times than I can count, I've turned over the straw, I've…"

"What do you mean they've gone? Where have they gone?"

"Basically they've dematerialized," said Paolo. "We know he's done it before, Ariel told us. He spontaneously emptied himself and the maggots pulled his skin out of a tiny hole. At the psychiatric ward."

"What about her?"

"Well, it looks like Houdini found his apprentice."

"You twat!" cried Giacomo and hung up.

34.

In spite of all the disasters that day, Giacomo's greatest regret was that he never had time to eat his custard roly-poly when it was ripe and ready. Many hours later he returned to it and recognized that its edges had dried and its custard coagulated like spoilt milk. A thing must always be enjoyed at the perfect moment. Delay imposed a sort of moral inversion on things: what was once considered a general good would become an evil.

Colonization, slavery, industrial development had all at times been considered by various fools and villains to be aspects of progress. Yet, when compared with these monstrous historical facts, Giacomo felt there could never be a compelling argument against a custard roly-poly.

The only argument was that it must be enjoyed.

And that was why he had a strong feeling of regret and sadness as he reached out and pressed the panic button. He knew that his peace was over. Maggot employees all over Rome would spring into immediate action. Intrusive telephones would start ringing everywhere, in the homes of off-duty personnel sitting quietly enjoying a syringe of heroin, or in bedrooms where they lay sleeping, or kitchens, where friends teemed around tables burgeoning with steaming plates. Giacomo licked his lips, filled with the sadness of abstention. What would they be eating? Maybe some grilled St. Peter's fish with olive oil and grated horseradish, or barbecued pig's trotters and bottles of home-distilled grappa?

How lovely and what a terrible waste. The feasting would be interrupted everywhere as a great number of irritated individuals pulled on their work clothes again and hurriedly set off.

Within an hour at most, hundreds of security men were swarming all over the depots, warehouses, blast-proof air locks, caverns, catacombs, bone-houses and lift shafts.

Michael and Ariel were gone without a trace.

The presence of two rogue maggots in the high security areas of the catacombs was unprecedented and considered highly dangerous.

Giacomo set up his operational HQ in the da Vinci Chambers—he even had his desk brought down from his office on the surface—complete with newly installed hotlines and TV monitors and CAD drawings of the one hundred and twenty-eight known levels of the Gnostic catacombs.

But, as he observed to Paolo, the place was just too enormous to search efficiently—over a mile and a half deep in places. It was even possible that the catacombs merged with natural cave systems that went deeper still to places that could only be plumbed by professional cavers.

At the end of that first day, Giacomo was debriefed by the head of security who had nothing much to say except that no one had been found and nothing discovered. The fugitives had *disappeared*. That word again.

Paolo had had the foresight to have a cooker installed, and an extractor fan. He was quietly boiling up some pasta in the background, too canny to open his mouth unless spoken to.

Giacomo let slip a long racking sigh and said, quietly. "Oh dear."

Paolo put down his wooden spoon and turned round. "Have they not found *anything*? A cigarette end? A splash of urine?"

"We're not looking for their DNA! This is not a police investigation!" snapped Giacomo. "No, we have nothing on them. We can't even say how big this place is—for all we know there's an enormous cave at the bottom with a dragon sleeping in it."

"Of course, all mysteries are bottomless," Paolo agreed with a sigh. "Consider this, my old friend: all this time we've been taking the living out of circulation and storing the best of them down here. But what if our day never comes? What if we never inherit our bright new world? If we end up as dust instead, buried under millions of tons of rubble?"

"As long as they don't get out of the Catacombs we'll be fine," said Giacomo. "I've posted guards at all the exits." He rubbed his face. "I just wish I knew why they've done this. I don't trust them; they're up to something and it's worrying me, I can feel an itch, Paolo, right here." He punched his chest.

"You don't think they'd talk to journalists, do you?"

"No, no," cried Giacomo. "Just concentrate on your pasta, Paolo. You don't understand. They don't need us; they don't want us. They can find themselves a farm to live on, grow their damned vegetables, breed their own maggots, and live without us… also without God. It sets a terrible precedent and it damages our plans. Everyone will know they made fools of us; people will laugh at us."

Paolo nodded soberly, not quite managing to suppress a satisfied grin as he took out his pièce de resistance from the fridge, a tub of Bolognese sauce that in his view rivaled anything available in Rome's best restaurants.

Giacomo was still on the rack of his worst imaginings. "They could also stir up a lot of trouble at the Vatican. They could talk to the Liaison Officer. And he'd have a good excuse to say we were incompetent. They could close us down; Lord knows we have enough enemies."

Paolo placed a bowl of spaghetti in front of Giacomo with a glass of sumptuous Barolo. Then he watched as Giacomo's expression of anguish slowly melted into a transported smile.

"Bless the bread," said Giacomo with a grateful nod, then, after a slurp, added, "and the wine."

The two friends ate in silence, while both thinking to themselves that if all failed, if they were hunted out of Rome like fugitives, then at least they would spend their lives munching their way through all the regions of Italy.

Their bliss was short-lived. Soon there was a commotion outside as a group of guards delivered Cardinal O'Hara—in handcuffs. He'd spent the last few hours being jostled from one cave to another by stressed-out security personnel, unsure in the general pandemonium about what to do with him.

"Leave him there," said Giacomo, who was now more or less restored. He pointed to an uncomfortable plastic chair in the corner, into which O'Hara was unceremoniously shoved.

For the next few hours, Giacomo and Paolo dealt with a stream of visitors—security personnel, geologists, Vatican officials.

Giacomo stood at his desk like some field marshal—or better still, Winston Churchill—poring over maps, pointing, giving orders, and occasionally downing a shot of Armagnac or hurriedly puffing on his cigar.

O'Hara envied him his power, his freedom to express himself; above all, his utter disregard for notions such as sin.

When all the briefings were over and done with, Giacomo turned to O'Hara and realized that his malingering presence had added a further note of sourness to the night—his constant chuckling from the corner.

Giacomo turned to a guard. "Would you be kind enough to remove this sack of shit, take him downstairs, and keep him under arrest? He's not to go anywhere until further notice." He looked at O'Hara. "I'm seriously considering letting you expire... keeping you out of our vaults so you can enjoy your precious mortality."

As O'Hara was brusquely removed from the room, he threw Giacomo a final lingering gaze, and thought to himself, "If there's any way I can give this man a painful death, I will."

This venal thought was a great comfort to him.

35.

When Michael and Ariel reached the ancient catacombs deep under the north transept of St. Peter's, they found no modern technology or forklift trucks, only dank, dripping passages and compacted silence, in a world where nothing ever moved. The catacombs were so vast that at times one wondered if they had even been made by humans. Yet it seemed safe to assume they had, for there were carvings everywhere, on every lintel and passage, with names and dates in Romanic numerals and occasionally birds, trees, or fish.

The windings of the various chambers were mostly by a sort of design, not intestinal in their shape but logical.

The first day they just wandered without purpose, descending another level whenever they chanced on cramped stairs winding down like a screw thread.

"Lucky we're not claustrophobic," said Ariel. "We'd scream the place down."

"I am claustrophobic," said Michael. "Every step I take I'm fighting panic."

Occasionally they were disturbed by search parties with powerful torches. Whenever they saw or heard anything, they stepped into the nearest side passage, of which there were hundreds, each immediately bifurcating, and then bifurcating again.

If by any chance their pursuers got too close, it was easy to clamber behind a stone sarcophagus and lie very still until they had passed. There were sepulchral niches cut into the rock on either side up to ceiling, and nicely proportioned spaces between the wall and the sarcophagi for hiding or getting a bit of sleep.

"There's nothing to bloody do down here, is there?" Ariel said after a few days of traipsing about. "Do we actually know why we're here? Otherwise we could end up walking around for years. And if we ever have the crazy notion of trying to get out of here, we'll meet plenty of helpful people at the top who'd like nothing more than to stuff our throats with embalming cloth."

"I thought that's what you wanted? To sleep?"

She looked at him. He'd grown so sharp and grim; his comments often hit their mark with an edge of cruelty. She swallowed her guilt, knowing that she had made him what he was.

"You know, if we really want to leave this place we can't head *down*, can we?" she said. "Are you sure you're trying to escape, Michael? Are you sure you're not just playing games with your friends, the graybeards?"

Michael trudged on, considering her question, and then answered: "I'm running because they're puffed-up frauds; I'm sick of their pomposity. They mystify the maggot and keep it secret; they use its power to make themselves stronger. They tell themselves they're the custodians of our future, Ariel, but they're only saving their own skins."

"You sound a bit like them. Maybe you should also grow a beard? I'm sure it'll turn gray if you wait long enough."

"I might have to. I don't have a razor."

Their conversation drifted like this, sometimes argumentative, often consoling, but always aimless. They kept moving for the sake of moving, never knowing where they were heading.

On the third day the passages broadened and they reached an ultramodern silo where the Sacred Tomb of Jesus was housed in a lead-lined cavern beyond yet another pair of blastproof steel doors.

The place was absolutely deserted.

They stood, a little awed, looking up at the doors, which were as tall as a three-story building.

"I've got news for you," said Ariel. "Hanging round caves for no particular reason… isn't my thing."

"We should go inside at least and have a look."

Ariel stared dubiously at the steel doors. "I'm not sure I want to. Something tells me once you go in there you're there for keeps." Despising herself even as she spoke, she went on: "I'm lost. I don't know what I want anymore. I don't even know if I should stand or sit. I miss fruit and sunlight and water."

Michael nodded at a familiar contraption fixed into the wall, an adjustable double-prong at the top and a retractable hose below. "At least we can top ourselves up when we need to." He wandered over to the machine, and stood there fingering the controls, while he thought back on the bullshit Mama Maggot had fed him when she emptied him in Sardinia. All that stuff about… what was it she'd called it?—the *passpartout*—and then the oath of loyalty she had made him swear.

Why did people with power always have to abuse it?

He tested the hose by touching the trigger. A high-pressure burst of wriggling maggots sprayed across the floor.

"Michael, leave that thing and come here."

She put her arms round him, kissed him and said, "When I am close to you I almost feel human. At least that's something I can be happy about."

"I'd say everything is going a bit too well," said Michael. "Maybe they actually emptied us and we're hanging up to dry and this is all a coffin dream? If it is, then I'm quite happy being dead."

36.

Giacomo woke up at six-thirty and made sure he was well tanked up on coffee, raisin rolls, Manchego cheese, and a half-bottle of Armagnac by the time his team of advisers turned up, showered and rosy-cheeked in their pressed suits.

One of the first things Giacomo did when he assumed his position as Grand Master of the Maggot Church was to have a group of top bankers and scientists maggotized and co-opted. He never bothered to learn their names; he didn't want excessive contact with seculars. They bored him, for one thing, and then of course they didn't qualify for storage and eternal life—which inevitably meant any friendship would have limited duration.

His chief statistician was a ferocious creature; he knew her simply as Chase, because that was the institution for which she had once worked. His financial analyst, a bit of a pompous dull-ard from South Kensington, went by the name of Barings. Then there was a smiling, voluptuous biologist, Smithsonian, who in another life would probably have had many happy children. Lastly, an acne-scarred information technology expert from New York—Warburg.

Giacomo watched them settling into their chairs, and as usual he marveled at their apparent ability to find pleasure in this whole ethos of *Don't fuck with us; we're here to do business and we know what we're talking about:* their salmon-striped cashmere suits, thousand-dollar handbags, polka-dot silk ties, expensive splashes of aftershave or perfume, the hiss of tights as legs were crossed, then those shoes, polished and sharp-heeled, lurking under the table like malevolent insects. Warburg, on the other hand, affected a sort of disheveled slacker appearance, always glum, always arrayed in a baggy tracksuit, long hair shedding a light rain of dandruff, a diamond stud in his left earlobe.

Giacomo frowned: Oh, blast it, it was just a lot of ego-posturing, the whole thing. The trouble was he needed them.

He cleared his throat. "I've called you in this morning because we must analyze the state of play. As you know we're having a problem with mortality; we're talking here about significant people—bishops, cardinals, proper religious people—dying without any prospect of ever coming back. It's never happened before."

"Could I ask … ah … you, whoever you are," he said awkwardly, glancing at Chase, "to give us a rundown of the situation."

"Certainly," said Chase with a repressed frown: "Guys, can I have the projector?" She stood up and walked up to the screen, showing a world map with all the countries color-coded according to their "maggot saturation."

Using her electronic pointer she clicked first on Beijing. "What we have is a statistical problem that's pretty damn complex, kind of interesting too…"

"Really?" scowled Giacomo. "What's so interesting about it?"

"Well, let's take an example. At current maggot levels available to the Beijing market it's going to take like two hundred and sixty-three years to neutralize the population."

"That's absurd," said Giacomo. "I've got ten or twenty years at most."

"Right," said Chase. "The problem we have, sir, is if we move more maggot product into the region we're looking at significantly higher maggot die-off levels. Even if we ram Beijing with five times more maggot, the projected timeframe only improves by…" Her face froze as her brain crunched into the equation: "…just short of a century."

"*That's absurd!*" roared Giacomo.

"Anyway, we can't move that much maggot into China, sir. There's a political issue. The Chinese secret service is onto us, and according to our information, they're starting up a maggot program of their own."

"The Americans are doing the same, and the European Union, too. The technology is very easy," Smithsonian cut in, with a lovely grin. "Any imbecile can breed them. All they need is oxygen and sugar. Let's just hope North Korea doesn't get hold of them."

There was a thunderous silence.

Chase continued. "The problem is the die-off factor. If we tried to blitz Beijing with a really massive program, say a tenfold increase, the maggots would actually die off before we got them there."

"What we've got here is a sort of entropy," Warburg whined. "If we could figure out the problem, we might be able to recalibrate the program and stabilize our targets. Or even modify the maggots… change their hard-wiring."

"But then we'd have to get into genetic engineering," Smithsonian sighed, with a look at Giacomo. "What does the Church feel about that?"

"I really couldn't give a fuck," said Giacomo irascibly. "I'm faced with a classic Patton-Montgomery conflict of interest." He stood up, grasping his cigar and bottle of Armagnac. "At the end of the Second World War, Churchill wanted to use Montgomery's armored brigades to punch aggressively through the lines of German resistance and race for Berlin. But the Americans insisted on Patton's lines advancing very slowly, taking out all the resistance as they went. And this is why we lost Eastern Europe to the Russians." He stopped, and swigged his Armagnac. "Just in case any of you have any doubts about where I stand, I want you to know I'm more of a Montgomery man, myself. That means I want the populations of Beijing, Mexico City, Kuala Lumpur, Bangkok, Los Angeles, Moscow, and New Delhi punched out within ten years... or I'll decommission you all... and I won't put you in coffins. I'll throw you in the fire."

He sat down.

Barings had been very quiet up until now. "Sir, what possible advantage would you gain by having us liquidated?" he said in a muted, gentlemanly tone. "Don't you see? This thing is quite out of our hands: the maggots are a force in their own right. To be frank with you, sir, we are doing our utmost. We have no choice but go along with..."

"Oh, shut up, you English prick!" said Giacomo. "Always the same posturing self-confidence. Don't expect me to be reasonable; I am not fucking reasonable at all. I've always hated your country, ever since that fat, gut-bucket king of yours murdered our brothers and took over our Church and spurted his sterile, diseased spunk into all those poor girls and then one by one had them murdered on the scaffold."

Barings went pale. "I'm not sure this is getting us very far... sir."

"I'll show you where it's getting you... you atheist *fuck*," said Giacomo, pressing a button under his desk. Immediately the door opened and a couple of security men walked in accompanied by a priest. Giacomo turned to them: "Take this man below, empty him, and put him in the incinerator. No, that's too severe," he muttered under his breath. "Put him in storage for a hundred years."

Barings stood up. "I simply don't understand," he wailed. "I've done nothing against you."

"There's no reward for that. You've done nothing *for* me," said Giacomo, "and that's what counts ... old chap."

"What about my family?"

"Don't you worry about them. I'm not a horrible man, I'll have them maggotized as well, then decommissioned. We'll reactivate them at the same time as you, how's that? When you wake up, my friend, you'll find a nice, clean, empty world without so many annoying people in it. It'll be quite lovely for your family; you'll see. But you'll have to take up gardening, because there won't be any banks and no money, either. Or boarding schools!"

Barings was led off weeping.

Giacomo tried not to look too smug as he refocused on his think-tank. By this time they were looking mesmerized and uncomfortable, like rats lined up in front of a python. "You see," he informed them pointedly, "my problem is I don't *like* most people very much. *People* don't seem to realize the world is an arena where God and the Devil are slugging it out. They think our planet is a place for humans to live, build factories, and drive cars. How very silly." He turned to the biologist: "Smithsonian… do you actually understand the significance of the problem we're facing? I need to get rid of the human race, quickly!" With a shake of his head, he refocused on her. "I mean you seem like a sweet woman; why on Earth didn't you just stay at home and get married?"

Smithsonian worked hard to control herself—she grew intense and positively glowed with resentment. "Isn't it enough for you that you took my life from me? Must you make me crawl on the ground? Do you understand what I've paid… my personal sacrifice for my liaison with you?"

Giacomo scowled. "Don't try to blag me, you silly bitch. I'm not concerned with your feelings. We're here to ensure that God wins the cosmic battle, and He will only do that if we sweep out the old, corrupt, secular institutions. Governments, for instance, have to go…" His eyes swept over his team as he addressed them: "I'm concerned that you people don't fully understand our program. Do you?"

There was universal agreement that they *did* understand. Very quickly, the meeting broke up with handshakes and spilled coffee and a lingering smell of exclusive aftershave.

As soon as he was by himself, Giacomo had a fit of remorse. Maybe those bloody Churchill memoirs he was reading had gone to his head? He sat there for a while, then picked up the phone and dialed an extension.

"Has Barings been done yet? Barings… or what's-his-name? That bastard I sent down. Has he been emptied yet?"

A weary voice at the other end informed him that what's-his-name had been emptied and hung up to dry five minutes ago, but could certainly be resuscitated, except the shift had just changed. Reversing the process would thus necessitate calling back the last shift, paying overtime, holding back the new shift in the service elevator and…

"Forget it," Giacomo cried and hung up.

The door clicked behind him and Paolo walked in. "I heard about your economist," he said. "I suppose you're regretting it already?"

"Yes. Of course. But what was I supposed to do? I'm a passionate man; I can't help it."

"Well," said Paolo, struggling with the seal of a jumbo-pack of pork scratchings, "you could control yourself."

"Ah, it's all too much. Old Nick is running rings around us," sighed Giacomo. "It's like watching Brazil playing Belgium in the semi-final. And we have problems in Beijing."

"In Beijing of all places?" said Paolo, munching. "Do we really care?"

"Paolo, the world is changing. The World of Matter is rising up to fight us. There's no long, slow ride down the hill for us, my old friend, no waiting little inn surrounded by olive trees. Oh, no. And certainly no glasses of cold beer on the table. It wouldn't surprise me if we end our days in an American prison, being waterboarded, having our asses interrogated off or flown around in planes to be tortured by Syrians."

"Well, I suppose technically speaking we're guilty of crimes against humanity," said Paolo. "Most of the people we send down to the stripping room will never open their eyes again; let's face it. There are too many maggots in the world. God wants to punish us and that's all there is to it."

"Pretty fucking disgraceful, aren't we?" Giacomo chuckled diabolically, then stopped and shot his friend an irritated look. "We're doing what we have to do, Paolo. That old word, *humanity*, that's what's causing all the trouble. When it boils down to it, who's really human anyway? Or humane, should I say? If people really cared about each other, they'd sort out their fucking *issues*, wouldn't they?"

"True enough," Paolo agreed.

"But they don't; they won't even admit there are any issues. Let me tell you, Paolo, Homo sapiens will sink into the abyss while watching television and eating a bag of potato crisps. And because Homo sapiens refuses to sort out the problems, we're going to have to do it for him. As for these prawn-eating, Rolex-wearing, Chinese simpletons, we can't just let them take over, can we? Cut down our forests, drill up our oil, and turn Eden into a filthified dump, all for the sake of their blessed Lear jets and hookers and Bentleys and Picassos. Idiots!" Giacomo sucked in air and calmed himself. "In the final analysis we'll be doing all the killing for humanitarian reasons."

The two men sat quietly watching the rising smoke of their cigars.

Then, articulating a thought common to them both, Paolo muttered, "I suppose Michael and Ariel felt they could live without our friendship." And then added wistfully, "In their place, I wouldn't have turned down the chance of a long sleep."

"There was something about that boy. How he got out of that cave I'll never know. Bloody miracle if you ask me."

"The odd thing is he doesn't even believe in God."

"It's awful, but I think God prefers him to the both of us, Paolo. We'd better start praying there isn't a heaven at all, because if there is I doubt we'll ever see it. Which makes our sacrifice even greater."

Paolo took him literally. "I agree. Let's go and pray for a while."

Reluctantly, Giacomo agreed.

The two men took the elevator up and, at the approach of midnight, eased their tired, millennial knees onto the venerable slabs of St. Peter's.

37.

Although it was half past two in the morning and Rome lay in deep mist, O'Hara was awake in his rib-shaped cell, clutching a bottle of single malt to his heart.

Outside the bars stood a hawk-like ecclesiast with an unpleasant intelligence about him as he perused the Irish renegade within. O'Hara kept pacing to and fro, compulsively swinging his head like a captive bear. His two-day stubble and too-much darting eyes did not impress. The ecclesiast, Sergio Rodriguez, was the Vatican's maggot liaison officer and a man of power. He had a condescending tone when addressing O'Hara, whom he viewed as damaged goods.

"Patrick, you've asked me here and I've come at considerable inconvenience, but, given the circumstances, I've tried to be obliging. My assumption, based on your own words, is that you… wish to talk about the problem of Monsignor Giacomo."

"Correct," said O'Hara savagely. "And I need your help… your authority… to start dealing with it in a forceful manner. Basically, he needs bumping off."

"Dear God, where do you think you are? We don't bump people off. We may in exceptional cases remove them, but that's quite different. Do also bear in mind that you're no longer one of our congregation. Technically, I no longer have jurisdiction over you." The liaison officer gave him a troubled, lingering stare. "You have joined the subterranean branch, Patrick; you have very publicly taken their vows and drunk from the Holy Grail and at this very moment you are in a devotional cell, preparing for enshrinement."

"Don't!" cried O'Hara, "Please don't use that damned word. Even linguistically I'm dead set against these people."

"I don't think they are so very concerned about that," Rodriguez observed drily.

"If we don't deal with this hooligan, he and his little friends will bleed us dry. The Church will fall into ruin."

"Oh, come now, the subterranean branch has always played its little apocalyptic games, neutralizing people here and there and hiding them in boxes. No one ever took it very seriously. This Giacomo is a gluttonous, simple man. As long as he's supplied with sucking pig and harlots he won't give us any trouble, you'll find."

"Are you aware of his plans for China?" O'Hara asked. "He's set on wiping it out. Also America."

Rodriguez's eyes flickered pedantically. "You mustn't put so much emphasis on people. Salt cod and virgin oil are purchased by the barrel, but people are not quantifiable numerically. Most of them are rotten, and many so deeply flawed that converting them to fertilizer is a rather attractive proposition, and also morally advisable. Don't you see this, Cardinal?" He waved his hands expressively, as if to introduce a note of practicality and logic. "I have to say in many respects I have a great deal of admiration for the maggot church. It is working its way through some of the world's most distasteful elements—criminals, drug addicts, tramps, refugees, prostitutes, squatters, and other ne'er-do-wells —removing them from circulation and taking away their ability to produce delinquent children. I might also add that His Holiness agrees with me, heavy though it is for him to admit it."

"Monsignor, I am sorry, but you are missing the point."

This time Rodriguez sucked in his breath and could not quite keep his composure, but before he could reopen his mouth there was a tap on the door behind him and his private secretary popped his head through. "Your Eminence, there's absolute mayhem upstairs. They're sending out search parties but they can't find Him. The cavern is empty and…"

"Oh, do go away! We already know all about this little Michael fellow," said O'Hara.

"I don't mean the young Englishman," said the secretary, turning to Rodriguez. "I mean Jesus! He's gone. His tomb's empty and they don't know where He is."

"How can that be?" Rodriguez propped himself up against the bars.

O'Hara saw hundreds of tiny bright lights dancing like fireflies in front of him. He grabbed Rodriguez and spat his booze-smelling words into his face: "I warned you, you stuck-up Spanish git. I told you to deal with that corrupt, fat swine. Why didn't you have Giacomo killed? Why?"

"In fact it was *your* job, wasn't it? And you failed," Rodriguez spat back.

O'Hara released his grip on the maggot liaison officer and took another slug at his bottle. "You never listened to me, did you? Oh no, you were always against me. Just because you could see others ridiculing me you had to do the same. You never had a mind of your own, you're a trivial little shit. You empty the pontiff's chamber pot and this makes you feel important. You'll go down in history as one of the idiots who misplaced our Shining Star, our Lord." He stopped to regain his breath, then opened his mouth wide and cried: "Whose responsibility was it to keep a close eye on the Maggot Church and ensure the safekeeping of our precious Holy Lord? It was yours, you snail-eating Spanish fuck. You failed to…"

But his sentence was cut short. While he'd been raging, Rodriguez had popped his head out of the door and ordered a guard inside to perform a little task.

O'Hara didn't see it coming.

He never had the vaguest presentiment of mortality as he launched into his attack on Rodriguez. Why not release his pent-up fury? He was finished anyway. This Spaniard was not ever going to see it his way. All that awaited O'Hara now, at best, was a return to Limerick, where he would spend his last days staring idly at the shamrock etched into the thick white foam of his pint.

When he looked up, something came whistling through the air, hitting him very hard in the face and knocking him over. He enjoyed a momentary, close-up perspective of the fibrous weave of a rug, which struck him as fascinating.

It occurred to him that he should have spent more time in his life looking at the tiny things.

38.

The resurrection of Jesus had taken place as follows:

On the third day of their vigil by the steel doors, Michael and Ariel had hidden in a side passage when they saw a procession of women in white robes moving towards them with lit candles. They shuffled along as if tranquilized—utterly catatonic, singing torpidly while their eyes gazed into infinity.

When the serpentine procession reached the steel doors, two stout Teutonic maids with tresses like golden loaves of bread stepped up to the scanners and pressed their palms to the glass screens.

There was a rumbling sound as the steel doors rolled aside for them like the waters of the Jordan.

Michael and Ariel had simply joined the tail end of the line as it curved into the Lord's chamber.

The women did not hang about once they got inside. Within seconds they were burning incense, sweeping, mopping, sprinkling the floor with essential oils and opening the Lord's sarcophagus and rubbing ointments into his skin.

Ariel grew conscious of a great inner turmoil. She sat down and pressed her palms against her temples. Thoughts bubbled up in her, and she would have loved to turn off what felt like a churning radio inside her head.

Michael seemed to be having the same problem. He paced about, muttering: "What do we do now? We have to do something."

Ariel closed her eyes and felt herself falling into a trance. She smelled damp soil under trees, heard wind rustling through overhead leaves. The physical world beyond this place, the wheeling stars, the operation of the Earth—these were the images that ran through her mind.

She felt something wriggling against her stomach, under her blouse. She unbuttoned herself. What she saw was a surprise, even to her.

A small hole had opened in the middle of her navel.

A fat, orange maggot wriggled out and lay against the lining of her trousers. She almost did not want to touch it. It had two black, glistening eyes and it seemed to be looking at her.

Ariel stood up and slowly advanced towards the sarcophagus where Jesus lay. The women stood aside to let her pass. She opened Jesus's mouth and placed the orange maggot on his tongue.

Within a few seconds, colour returned to the sallow, pale cheeks. His eyes swiveled and opened. They were light brown, like sandalwood. The speed at which the body refilled itself was nothing short of miraculous.

By the time the women had filed out of the chamber, still singing, Jesus was rising out of his sarcophagus. He stepped out and brushed the dust off his cloak.

His hair had been combed and oiled every week for two thousand years, and his face massaged and moisturized. He looked like a normal man in his early thirties, who hadn't had his hair cut for a good while.

"Follow me," said Jesus, who seemed to know exactly what he was doing. He walked briskly to an elevator, which he called down even though it was locked and alarmed. The doors opened smoothly and they all stepped inside.

A few minutes later they were back on the surface, walking through a crowded street in Rome. After the darkness of the caves, the bright streets filled them with wonder. The sun beat down, transforming every crumbling façade, every weather-beaten face.

"What do we do now?" Michael whispered to Ariel.

"I don't know. We follow him."

They looked at the figure of Jesus in front of them. He was walking briskly, a certain amusement in his eyes as he took in the urban scene: the cars, the aircraft passing over.

They stopped off briefly at a cash machine, which spasmodically spat out money until they had more than they needed.

As they walked away, money lay scattered on the pavement behind them.

"We must leave this place," said Jesus, "and get to the mountains. I have no business in the city among these empty buildings. We need a large chariot to take us away."

Quickly they dived into a taxi, asking to be taken to a mobile home showroom on the outskirts of Rome. Within an hour, they had bought a gleaming air-conditioned camper van with a galley kitchen, two separate sleeping cabins at the back, and a bathroom with a small Jacuzzi.

Jesus sat quietly in an upholstered sofa staring out of the window as they drove out of Rome.

"It's good to be back in the world," he said, smiling jauntily at them.

"It must be, my Lord, after all the time you spent sleeping," said Ariel politely.

"Time doesn't mean a thing. Time is one of your little inventions," said Jesus. "Please stop calling me Lord, would you? I have no desire for any sort of veneration. Certainly it is true I'm not actually a human being at all, yet I'd prefer it if you treated me as one."

Michael cleared his throat and said, tentatively: "Ah... Jesus? Would you like to hear some music?"

"Yes. Please. I want music. Of course."

Michael slotted one of his newly bought CDs into the player. Bob Dylan's wailing harmonica kicked off, filling the whole bus with the first few bars of *Stuck Inside of Mobile with the Memphis Blues Again.*

Jesus tapped his foot to the beat.

Outside, the landscape was changing. The camper was gliding through low-slung hills covered in holm oak and wild olive trees. The days down in the dark had left their mark on Michael's spirit—and this shadow had given much needed definition to him. Now free again, and with Jesus Christ safely on board, he felt something had been achieved, although it wasn't quite clear what.

Ariel was in the galley kitchen knocking up some lunch. "Anyone for an omelet?" she called out gaily. She was also very glad to be back on the road.

"Give me wine, woman," said Jesus. "And a soft-boiled egg."

And so she did.

39.

That night, after the enormity of recent events, Giacomo had great trouble sleeping. First, he lay for a good while thinking about Michael, Ariel, and Jesus, this improbable runaway trinity. Then, as his thoughts turned to other things, he realized why his life had become unbearable and, as a consequence, he had also become unbearable to himself.

Giacomo had become a weather vane turning in the wind, with no identifiable will or emotion of his own.

In one of his earlier lives he had spent some years in a lovely brick gatehouse to a mansion belonging to the estate of the Dukes of Bedford in Bloomsbury, London. At that time, Bloomsbury was a mature woodland of elm and oak, a peaceful bird-haunted place where one occasionally glimpsed a woodcutter with his nag or a party of horsemen looking for a fox or an otter to kill.

Giacomo had a wife who dressed with great care and strolled through the woods in silk slippers and painted lovely watercolors and spent her time talking to the maid or scrutinizing the quality of the Sunday roast. She was a collector of acorns and beechnuts, from which she made collages; also of shadow puppets, which she cut from sheaves of card he bought for her in Piccadilly.

Mostly they dined with the Duke, whose son Giacomo was tutoring in Latin and French.

Children they could have none, but there are some who believe that children are nothing but peace-shattering horrors. Giacomo and his wife had convinced themselves that this, without exception, was true.

Looking back, Giacomo had always felt this was his golden age.

He and his wife managed their business well. Every month or so a message was brought to their door from Rome, usually by night. Giacomo was not greatly taxed until the Gnostic Church in Rome ordered him to recruit the Dukes of Bedford, first by seducing one of the daughters who, as it happened, was no older than fourteen. Later there was a plot to maggotize the Duke and his oldest son. Giacomo happened to be on good terms with one of the most widely admired women in London, a mistress of a great number of fashionable men and also the finest procurer the maggot church ever had, with skin like milk and an agile, saucy tongue that swiftly brought men to their knees. The Duke was no exception.

His success with the Bedford family did not go unnoticed. Before long, a bunch of ambitious crackpots in Rome had involved Giacomo in a plot to maggotize the King of England. The Pope got wind of it, of course, and Giacomo was hauled before a hanging judge in the Vatican, who sentenced him to immediate termination. His wife was "spared," an odd term to use in view of the horrific poverty that she had to endure while he slept. She was permitted to stay on in the Bloomsbury gatehouse, but she earned a pittance as a seamstress and supplemented her diet with milled bark and wood sorrel. By the time Giacomo was reactivated about a hundred years later, he could not find her anywhere. He searched all over London, now entering the industrial revolution. The peasants had been transformed into swarming workers, covered in coal dust and with a raging fondness for gin.

Bloomsbury had declined. Mud and filth and weaving factories had spread where once there was greenery. In another three hundred years it would be turned into an urban cesspit filled with buses and drug addicts and Chinese tourists. No one would work there anymore; in fact, no one would work anywhere. This was the popular way of defining prosperity: ancient woodlands and farming communities turned into wastelands of boarded-up factories patrolled by drunks and lunatics, while, on a green hill behind electric fences, a small group of petty princes sat in stone houses and pontificated on the science of wealth creation, also known as *economics*.

No one should live longer than a thousand years. At a certain point it becomes impossible to remember anything at all. Only the hunger remains, the ravenous need to love and be loved, to eat and fill one's body or lose one's mind in chemical distraction.

The only thing Giacomo was still properly aware of was his unquenchable appetite. As far as he was concerned, nothing could take away the omnipotence of a fried egg.

Christianity was a ludicrous creed to him now. He was more interested in how to make a perfect hamburger. All the theology, all the doctrinal lisping had become a burden: raving madmen arguing about whose god was the best, like football supporters at a match, shouting abuse at their opponents.

Once an idea had turned into a burden it was time to let it go.

Only the other day he'd been walking along with a bottle of mineral water in his hand. When he tired of holding it he drank the water and discarded the bottle. Afterwards, it occurred to him that although he was still carrying the water in his body, its weight had somehow disappeared.

And like this it was also with ideas: they had to be a part of us.

In 1988 he had tracked down his wife to Berlin, where she was working as a professor at the Humboldt Institute. By this time she'd also developed a multiple personality. Her ego had grown; she was no longer a budding twig but a many-armed tree trunk floating ponderously down a river. She had learned to be skeptical of him, the man who had thrown away their happiness for the sake of personal ambition. Elegantly she showed him the door. His humiliation was crushing: he threw her a last lingering look as he gripped the doorknob.

"Why are you giving me that blank, self-pitying look?" she'd said. "You can't love what you don't love, Giacomo. I give you nothing as payment for what you have given me—also nothing…"

"So it meant nothing?"

"Whatever it meant then, is not what it means now. That is all you need to know."

Those words had festered for many years. But, recently, he had felt them raging in his blood with a new keenness. Giacomo had understood that his affection for Michael was largely rooted in his identification with him: Michael was doing what Giacomo ought to have done. Michael had given free rein to his personal ambition, in the sense of allowing himself to *feel*.

Michael did not want to sleep; Michael wanted to stay in the moment and not lose what he had. In other words he was not behaving as a proper maggot ought to. And this was problematic. Or, as Charles Darwin might have observed, it was an interesting aberration, a mutation that could lead to evolutionary development.

Giacomo had wanted to keep Michael safe and rolled up in a box until, at some point, many centuries into the future, he had the leisure to question him about it. How had Michael, who had no wisdom or experience, known with such certainty what he must do? Giacomo had never had any such conviction. Only confusion, confusion like mist on a heath.

The past leaned over him now, like the shadow of an unknown, possibly dangerous, figure in a doorway. Giacomo was a man suffering "the effects of memory," as he sometimes put it. And memory could not be revisited. Memory was a reunion dinner at which all the guests were strangers to one another.

To the City

40.

Waking from terrible dreams, Giacomo got out of his bed and put on his morning gown, went to the window and parted the curtains. He stared out at the bleak morning, the light drizzling rain.

For the first time in many, many days, he tried to say a prayer.

"Oh Lord…" he began, then stopped. Summoning whatever calm he had left, he opened the bedroom door and shuffled down the long, slightly dirty corridor that ended in a swing-door leading into the kitchen, where he found Günter already sitting on a chair with his ears pricked.

Paolo was at the gas cooker, portioning out a greasy fry-up on large dinner plates.

Giacomo's eye fell on three buckets of writhing white maggots, lined up against the wall. "What in the world is *that*?" he said weakly. "Shouldn't they be kept covered?" He went to the sink, wet a couple of tea towels and threw them over the buckets.

"First have your breakfast," Paolo muttered. "Then we'll fill you in on all the details."

"I had awful dreams," Giacomo mumbled. "All this trouble is getting the better of me. I think I'm losing my reason. I was back in Bloomsbury all night."

"Never mind about that. The maggot liaison officer called first thing this morning," said Paolo. "He's given us until midday to leave Rome or we'll be killed."

Giacomo listened as he devoured his crispy bacon rashers. After he'd stilled his worst hunger pangs, he asked Paolo whether he'd been to St. Peter's that morning.

"Of course, I went first thing," said Paolo. "I met Günter on the way. We popped into a favorite bar of mine, had a few artichoke fritters and a couple of espressos, and were slightly delayed as a result. We realized something was wrong as soon as we got there. There were lorries on the west side unloading construction materials. Must have been thirty or forty workers there. They'd screened off the whole area so the tourists couldn't see what was happening. There was an absolute profusion of security guards everywhere. We went through the cordon and ran into a crowd of maggots who hadn't been allowed into the crypts. The doors were barred. I demanded to know what was going on. I spoke to the foreman and he took me inside. Paolo stopped. "You won't believe it."

"Tell me."

"They'd chalked a line across the main reception. Anyone on the inside of the line wasn't allowed to leave."

Günter gave a little bark of excitement: "There were two men lying dead on the floor. Martyrs. Shot through the head. Very accurately done."

"The construction workers were drilling holes in the floor and inserting reinforcement rods across the whole vestibule. They put up a sturdy wood partition. Outside I heard the cement mixers churning and grinding."

"The guards moved us out; a few of them had their guns ready to stop anyone on the other side of the line from leaving."

"Before we knew it there was liquid cement being pumped in."

"They plugged the entrance, basically. Block by block. Hundreds of tons of cement. We stood there listening to the shouting from the other side of the concrete wall. It grew increasingly faint."

Günter took over: "When the shouting stopped we heard…"

"Singing," said Paolo, "They started singing." He blew his nose and looked at Giacomo. "If I hadn't been slightly late because of the artichoke fritters, I would have been on the other side of that chalked line. I would have been buried alive like the rest of them. I owe my life to some artichoke fritters; isn't that ridiculous?"

"Yes," said Giacomo, who felt curiously unaffected. "It is."

Günter picked up the thread. "While the wall was being built, we noticed a few brothers waving at us from the other side of the line. They'd brought up fresh maggot from the vaults." He nodded at the buckets lined up against the wall. "They passed them across when the guards weren't looking."

"Their courage was exemplary," said Paolo. "One of them tripped and fell. He went into the cement, just sank into it like quicksand."

There was a long silence. Giacomo wondered at his lack of empathy until he reminded himself that empathy was not one of his strengths. "So," he said. "There must have been a decision from the top to close us down." He stood up, went to the kitchen cupboard, and started stuffing his specialties—Ligurian pine nuts, Sardinian anchovy fillets, salted capers, dried chilies—into a cotton sack. "We've caused too much trouble. They'll take control and assert proper centralized authority. It's this whole business of the runaway Christ that's got the wind up them."

Only when he sat down did the enormity of it overwhelm him. "You know what this means, don't you? It means O'Hara, the shit, actually put an end to us when he planted Michael in our midst."

"Oh, that little innocent had nothing to do with it."

Paolo nodded. "I have to say I agree. But I'd give my eyeteeth to know how he managed to get out of that cell. And find Jesus."

"And rouse him," said Günter. "Who would have thought it?"

Giacomo looked at his watch again. "So we have to be out of Rome in just under three hours. Does that give us enough time to pack?"

"Pack what, in the name of God?" said Paolo. "I shall just bring my Bible and my walking boots."

"The only thing I own is my collar," said Günter.

"We have to find a suitable container for the maggots," Giacomo said. "From now on we'll take one or two every morning."

Günter yawned. "I'm ready for a little peregrination. The gardens of Bonus Pastor are starting to look a little dull."

Paolo looked at Giacomo: "And where should we go?"

"I own a nice little monastery in La Spezia," said Giacomo. "We'll wait there until Jesus surfaces. His presence won't go unnoticed. At some point we'll have to go and see… Him… and persuade… Him… to turn Himself in."

"Sounds funny, when you put it like that," said Günter.

"It may sound funny," Giacomo growled. "But it isn't."

He swallowed two maggots as if they were vitamin pills and bid the others do the same. They poured the maggots into large plastic containers, after perforating the lids and placing rotten bananas inside.

At exactly twelve o'clock they boarded a train. Giacomo and Paolo were carrying hefty rucksacks, loaded with food, maggots, and a change of clothes.

A group of unsmiling men at the barrier, obviously Vatican agents, spoke into their walkie-talkies as the train pulled away. Giacomo saluted them, as if making light of their presence. But he quickly brought his arm down. When he looked at his wrist it seemed as if there was a leash clipped to it, a leash effortlessly fed out from an infinite, many-geared spool in Rome.

I'll never get away from them, he thought.

41.

A few weeks after their departure in the camper bus, Michael and Ariel took stock of their experiences so far. While it could not be denied that Jesus had some sort of power, the Master remained deeply enigmatic to them.

At his bidding, they had driven all over Europe: along valleys, up hills, and through tunnels, across bridges and over plains. No matter how far they drove it was never quite enough for Jesus, who mostly sat at the back of the camper bus drinking goat's milk (which he was terrifically fond of) and methodically working his way through Michael's newly acquired CD collection. "Keep going, keep going," he'd call out, waving his arm. "Farther, farther…"

At first they had been patient. After all, they didn't know what Jesus was looking for or where he was intending to go.

"But where? Where now?" they'd call out and Jesus, closing his eyes as if in deep concentration, would say, quietly, "Vienna," or "Zurich." And so the haphazard journey continued.

It was almost as if Jesus was intent on seeing every motorway in Western Europe. Even ring roads did not escape his rapt interest: Frankfurt, Berlin, London, and Paris were all circumnavigated, and service stations sampled for their cafés and shops.

"Jesus, do you actually *like* pizza?" Michael asked once, as they sat at a red Formica table one evening on the outskirts of Hamburg.

"Liking or not is unimportant. I need to eat a pizza so I know what a pizza is, and once I know what it is I can then decide if it is good or not," said Jesus. "But for my part it seems little more than bread and meat. In my day there would have been little call for it, although outside the temple or the market there were usually one or two vendors' stalls." He shrugged. "They sold *fava* beans and chopped herbs or perhaps liver or falafel. People were less prepared to waste money in those days. Every piece had value. But they were fond of tittle-tattle even back in my day; they did not have televisions and not newspapers, either. So they liked to gossip instead." With an amused smile he held up a celebrity magazine and shook it in the air. "Rihanna," he said. "She seems a nice little girl; what a pity to give her so much attention."

At night, when they retired to their bunks, Jesus would lie in his bunk singing along to whatever music was playing on his portable hi-fi. His favorites were Bob Dylan, Mississippi John Hurt, and Janis Joplin, but he also had a sneaking regard for early U2 and knew most of their songs by heart.

He seemed impervious to boredom. He could spend all day throwing dice or rearranging some peanuts in a bowl.

There were days when Michael looked at him and thought to himself, "Is this the same Jesus who changed the history of the world?"

Even Ariel, with her customary good humor, found little to entertain her in the garish sweet shops where they spent hours so that Jesus could stock up on magazines and chocolate.

His interest in minutiae was enormous. For instance, he was capable of reading food labels almost infinitely, wanting to know what folic acid was, or emulsifier, E331, Omega 3, and B6.

Tension was building up.

Ariel started snapping at Michael. "Don't be so bloody presumptuous," she told him. "The Master has a plan, and we don't know what it is. Not yet. We have to be patient."

"But what's the bloody plan? Eating sweets is not going to do much good, is it?" he protested. "I just wish I could understand."

Only once did Jesus allay Michael's doubts. He put his hand on Michael's shoulder and said, "You think you must do something. But you are a mechanism, my friend. You think work is done by turning the handle. I tell you, this handle you turn with so much energy is not attached to anything; it merely spins in the air, and the machine remains idle in spite of everything you do."

One morning as they lay in their bunks like sailors becalmed in the middle of some ocean, Jesus opened his eyes and sat bolt upright in his bunk.

"Enough of this," he said. "Time to go south."

His words brought immense relief. Immediately the trade winds seemed to stir among their idle sails. They were parked in a truckers' lay-by just west of Strasbourg, close enough to the nearside motorway lane to feel a slight tremor every time a roaring juggernaut passed on the other side of a narrow skirt of what looked like plastic trees. The landscape on both sides of the motorway was more or less flat to the edge of the horizon and seemed productive only in so far as it was covered in short, green blades of chemically enhanced growth.

Over their heads hung an indistinct gray sky too inert even to produce rain. Its sole purpose was to bathe the planet in a murky, wearisome light.

Michael turned the ignition and hoped there would not be too many detours on the way.

As they headed south, Jesus did not often move from his up-holstered sofa by the window. By now he'd amassed a great pile of books and magazines which he flicked through, occasionally looking up and analyzing the scenery outside. Or asking impossible questions. He tended not to be moralistic, but occasionally his sensibilities were hurt by something he saw or read.

Once, while flicking through a copy of *Vogue*, his face contorted with pain and he said, "So a supermodel is considered more beautiful than other women, is she?" Then frowning, added, "Young women always have beauty because they are loaded with physical destiny. But this beauty cannot be captured on a photographic plate; everybody knows this. The makers—so many makers you have in this world of yours—persevere with the impossible task because they can't think of anything else to do with their weary hands."

Another time he commented on some lyrics by Bob Dylan:

> *"But he just smoked my eyelids*
> *And punched my cigarette…"*

"This Bob is correct in his thinking," said Jesus, smiling with recognition as if he had come across a kindred spirit. "Sometimes the thing that *is* can only be described by saying exactly what it is *not*."

"Actually, that's just the Chicago School of Disembodied Poetics. There's nothing very profound about it," said Ariel. Jesus told her she was mistaken. Most so-called profundity was about as illuminating as a cowpat in the grass. And yet, he added, when one actually considered a cowpat in the grass it was not as simple as it seemed. Who would have thought that, in some obscure corner of the universe, a large hairy four-legged beast would lift its tail and deposit a lump of digested organic material on the ground?

Frequently his words were obscure or there seemed to be very little method in his ramblings. "Well, what did you expect?" Ariel whispered to Michael one night after the Master had gone to sleep. "I mean nobody actually knows what he was like. The people who told his story were basically poets or mystics—maybe they just liked a decent yarn and they jazzed it up a bit? Whatever happened in Palestine two thousand years ago has been mythologized."

The days passed and still Jesus did not reveal his intentions, thus prompting the question: was this just an extended sightseeing trip?

One day in the south of France, Jesus spent the afternoon walking, singing, and watching clouds while Ariel and Michael sat in the camper bus playing cards. When Michael articulated his disquiet, Jesus looked at him sternly and for the first time Michael felt directly challenged by his words:

"How can I give you purpose, a thing you will not give yourself nor even ask for?"

"I'm sorry," said Michael. "I don't mean to be presumptuous. I just want to know if there's a plan."

"Plans are for fools."

Later that night, when Michael and Ariel lay in their double-bunk, Michael wondered about his purpose in life. He tried to explain his hopes and dreams to Ariel, but he found to his own surprise that he had none—although he didn't admit so much to her. Ariel listened with interest although it was abundantly clear to her that Michael was a typical twenty-first century man with an ethos of materialism as the oxygen of his blood.

Besides, the very notion of "a dream" had something plasticized about it. Dreams were mostly actions involving a purchase: an airline ticket, a house, a horse, some land. Michael's generation did not say, "I am a player of the drums; hear me." Michael's generation said, "I want to buy a drum kit." Having acquired the physical, defining object, there was the whole problem of turning oneself into someone else, a rock star, film director, deep-sea diver, astrophysicist, martial arts expert, poker player, tycoon.

In practice, ideas were far more interesting and accessible as nuggets of speculation than the grind of their attainment.

After listening to Ariel's arguments, Michael told her he wanted to live on a farm, grow vegetables, keep animals, and learn some carpentry. She found herself slightly disheartened.

"What you're describing is nothing. It's not a dream."

He sat up on his elbow and stared at her. "What is it, then?"

"A description."

"Well, in that case I don't have any dreams."

"Good. Be honest. Spit it out. Life is bloody meaningless. The only things people actually like, and I agree with them, is dancing and making love. That only works while you're young.

Everything else is a bore from beginning to end." She sighed deeply, glancing towards Jesus's cabin, where the lights were still on.

Since that luminous day outside the Master's tomb in the catacombs, their sexual intimacy had once again died a slow death. A feeling of ennui had begun to permeate their hurried lovemaking whenever Jesus left the camper bus for one of his meandering walks.

That night, Michael had nightmares about Ariel dying all over again.

In the morning when they woke up, Jesus was standing over them, squinting down at them with a slightly bemused expression on his face. "You're only here for the struggle to live," he said. "Not to mystify or complicate."

He put his hands on Ariel's temples and looked into her eyes. "Busy yourself," he said. "Accept my gift."

And to Michael he said "Rise into the light, my umbrageous son. Go forth."

That same evening they crossed the frontier and made their way down tiny roads into the Pyrenean massif, until they found a remote valley with a crumbling, semi-abandoned village at one end. The road climbed to the top of a steep hill covered in scree.

"Park it here," said Jesus. "Park it straight and well, for it shall never move again."

Michael was puzzled, but he did as he was told.

Over the next few days he followed with growing interest the news bulletins on their radio and television, brought to them courtesy of the satellite dish on the roof of their vehicle. The world had started picking itself apart while they had been loafing about in Europe. Stock exchanges everywhere were in meltdown because of malfunctioning computers. Scientists were being hired to solve the problem, but the problem was not in the programming or the hardware. The problem, in the words of one fascinated Nobel laureate, was that "the logos has changed;

the laws of the universe have scrambled themselves so that we have to reinvent mathematics, physics, and chemistry using a new set of rules." It seemed beyond their capacities and they admitted as much.

Banks were having problems establishing what monies were held in their deposits. Customers didn't know from one day to another whether they were millionaires or paupers.

Cars wouldn't start.

Aircraft had turned into dinosaur-proportioned lumps of metal no more likely to fly than stones.

Even power stations refused to generate electricity. In effect they had become very large, wasteful log fires pumping heat into the night, and there seemed little point in turning them on at all.

Everywhere there was a run on candles and paraffin. Junk shops were raided for brass lamps and candlesticks.

Gardens were ploughed up and turned into vegetable patches.

A crisis meeting of the G8 was convened. The gold standard was reintroduced about one hundred years after it had been phased out. The banking system was reformed. Letters of conveyance would henceforth be used rather than electronic transfer, which no longer worked. Hundreds of thousands of clerks were employed to write out balance sheets, copy documents, and manually post all correspondence.

The whole notion of trading in shares had to be abandoned.

In spite of enormous efforts to underpin the system, money lost its value. In the newspapers there was a lot of clever talk about "the new Weimar Republic." People would rather have a bag of potatoes than a pile of money.

Meanwhile, in silos all over the world, missile systems lay moldering, and tanks, aircraft and rifles were mothballed.

The "travel industry," as it had once politely been named, was disbanded overnight. No one was willing to take the risk of going on holiday, in case they were unable to come home again.

The available modes of transportation were also so limited that from then on, a "holiday" was usually something one undertook with a tent on one's back and a pair of walking boots on one's feet.

"Out of service" became a commonplace sign, posted here, there, and everywhere.

Armies, called out on the streets to maintain order, found themselves impotent to stop looting and fighting—although such tendencies were almost nonexistent. Before long, even elite regiments had been disbanded. There was nothing to pay them with anyway. And besides, their guns and missiles were so cranky that it was pointless pretending that they had a use on the battle-field. Even that word, "battlefield," became quaint and archaic.

National newspapers were no longer published as there was no effective way of distributing them. Only local newspapers were printed in small editions, and then delivered by urchins on bicycles.

Credit card companies, lending institutions and other financial bodies simply disappeared overnight. Records no longer existed, and governments everywhere discovered the awful truth: it was not possible to maintain control over the populace without recourse to the silicon chip.

These changes were global, immediate and universal.

About a week after they had arrived, Michael found one morning that neither his radio nor his television worked.

Jesus watched as Michael stood there cursing, flicking the buttons of his remote. Eventually he commented with a slight note of hilarity: "Do you miss it, Michael? Can't you use your own eyes and ears?"

Michael stared at Jesus, his long, unkempt locks framing his face, his long lean arms with the sinewy biceps and triceps, and, on his left inside forearm, the tattooed symbol of a fish. "Did you do this, Jesus?"

But Jesus never answered direct questions. They seemed to amuse him, as if they were somehow off the point. "It's not what I do that matters," he said. "The world has changed, it is true. But do you really have time to wonder why? Do you not have enough troubles of your own? The question is, what are you going to do today?"

He went outside and waved at a group of peasants coming up the hill with a horse. Soon they were at work, plowing.

As Michael stood there watching their plowshare opening a long gash in the ground, it occurred to him that this—the plow, the sweat of labor—was the only thing there had ever been. Everything else had been an illusion, and the illusion had passed.

While he and Ariel had been agonizing and theorizing, Jesus had enlisted groups of loyal followers. Men built hundreds of shelters or prepared the soil for planting. Women sheared sheep, spun wool, picked fruit, baked and slaughtered and brewed enormous quantities of beer. Jesus liked to sit in the evenings sharing a tipple with the hundreds of people who seemed to be living with them.

Michael did not enjoy his own skepticism, nor could he deny his conclusion: that Jesus had somehow dismantled all the apparatus of the modern world, and now that it had all gone, they would henceforth have to live like peasants intent only on the simplest of tasks—and the reality of wind and rain.

The other weird thing was that the maggots had grown rather sedate. They were content to vegetate, it seemed.

Both Michael and Ariel felt themselves settling into torpid, bloodless indifference; they asked themselves if Jesus had increased their happiness or merely blunted their appetite for life?

Their question did not go unanswered.

Jesus was aware of their predicament. Even as they began to enjoy a certain preeminence, as the hundreds of people turning up in the valley began to treat them with a deference apparently due to His closest people, even as they were recognized as the ones who shared His camper van and might therefore be party to special insights and wisdom, and even as Jesus's fame began to grow in a world where news no longer travelled so speedily, Michael and Ariel were caught up in disaffection.

Ariel, watching Jesus at work with the peasants, commented once to Michael, "So, what will the Vatican do now? The Messiah has a Protestant work ethic."

Jesus, who seemed to know everything, referred to Michael and Ariel as "my brooding friends," and one evening he deepened his definition, when he turned to Ariel over the fire and said, "Ariel, my dear woman, joy is a flower for your windowsill, not a nettle to be grasped."

She replied, "To me it's always been a nettle."

Jesus smiled quixotically and with his bare hand picked a burning log out of the fire and held it firmly in his hand. "Do I blame the log for the pain I feel?" he said, as the flames licked up his arm. "Or do I let it go? Do I give up on my hopeless expectations?"

He stood up and flung it as far as he could; in the night it traced a long, glowing arc across the sky.

"It sounds so easy when you put it like that."

"Ah," Jesus said rhetorically, "she wallows in malcontent while tacitly admitting the ease with which she might let go of her fears."

"I'm not happy here, not even with you, Master. I never wanted to live like a farmer. I'm a modern woman; I like home design and shopping and..." she added slightly idiotically, "I always wanted children."

Jesus seemed in a mood for preaching tonight. His jaws moved in a well-oiled and frothing manner. In the corner of her eye she noticed the shadowy figures of peasants quietly creeping up to the edge of the firelight, sitting there with their shining, magnetized eyes, their calloused hands and sprouting, greasy beards. Jesus included them in his conversation. His eyes scanned their faces and he raised his voice so that they could

all hear. "Yet her worries are not as she imagines. She confuses
the physical with the mental and does not realize that she is a
creature of ash, wood, and earth... a creature whose corruptions
can only be expelled through will. She is a shepherd of rats. She
minds her flock while lamenting the fact that rats are no good
to her; their fur is useless for wool and their meat is diseased. So
why does the shepherdess not go to market and fetch a ram and
a ewe for herself. Why does the shepherdess not create the thing
she requires?"

Jesus's eyes seemed to have grown, and the silence of the night
bent around them like a huge bell, amplifying the sound of his
voice.

From his pocket the Master took a pack of colorful balloons,
bought some weeks earlier in a service station. Solemnly he gave
one of the balloons to Ariel and indicated she should blow.

As she did so, a stream of charred, dead maggots came out
of her mouth and filled the balloon.

Jesus took it from her and released the heavy balloon into
the air. Amazingly, in spite of its weight it seemed impervious to
gravity, floating up until caught in a high breeze. As it rose above
the ridge across the valley, the unseen sun illuminated it, and it
became a tiny globule of fire as it disappeared into the west.

"If you want children, go and have children," he said. "Open
the door that waits for you. Enter your house."

42.

Soon Ariel began to note something changing in her body, and she realized she was pregnant. How this was actually possible she did not know. Had she really expelled the maggots from her body? Or were they sustaining the child in some sort of subcutaneous pocket?

Michael also went through revolutionary changes. He grew fitter and leaner, and as autumn set in he spent his days picking olives with the others. Michael and Ariel and others spread nets under the trees. After harvesting, they pruned errant branches and prepared for next year's harvest. Slowly, week by week, they picked all the olives in the valley and watched the rich oil dribbling out of the presses into twenty-liter glass bottles.

It occurred to Michael that now that they had oil, wine, and grain all earned from the hard-won ground, they were rich.

In the evenings, Michael and Ariel lay by their fire, resting after their long days. They longed for this child growing inside her. Often they sat with Jesus, relishing his silence.

The camper bus had become almost iconic. In the night it seemed to tower there at the top of the hill, like some many-tiered keep of stone, surrounded by hundreds of smoking fires.

One evening Jesus looked at them, his bearded leonine chin outlined against the flames as he spoke: "Soon your friends will come… more malcontents…"

"Who?" asked Michael.

"Oh, Romans, concerned with their position, as always; heavy laden with badges and laurels," said Jesus. "Here they will only find work, no feather beds."

"Do we know them?"

"Yes. One of them was once a friend of yours. He dug holes in the ground and made a resting place for the dead. I once slept there myself."

"Giacomo?"

"The same."

"What do they want?"

"They are Pharisees. They believe in gods of their own making, make rules for others to follow, harness the power and keep it for themselves."

Jesus placed a raw hen's egg in the fire and watched it with a half-smile. When it exploded, scattering egg white in all directions, he looked up and smiled. "The rooster sits on the egg, and a chick emerges. Without her soft breast, fire consumes all things and makes them worthless."

Ariel touched her stomach and Michael put his hand there, too.

Jesus continued. "Soon I must leave. But this is of little consequence to you or anyone else. You will remember me no less than our other friends who have lived with us here, in our home."

They were shocked by his words. Why this sudden departure, and what would they do without him, their Master?

"My work was not so much with you," said Jesus. "Not with Man. I will judge neither Man nor Woman. Let the truth speak for itself… if it has tongue to speak." His craggy face stared into the fire, weary. "I came to stop the juggernaut, and now I have. People have stopped moving and the fumes and poisons of their lives and minds are no longer killing their gardens. Now they must work to keep themselves alive."

"What about the sick and dying? Without all the medicines and hospitals, how will they be helped?"

"Have no fear, they will be helped."

After that, he would say nothing else. The night passed in a heavy, semi-conscious silence bursting with unanswered questions.

In the morning there were three distant figures coming up the hill: Giacomo, Paolo, and Günter. Jesus was cutting wood. He didn't even look up, merely glanced down the valley and wiped his brow.

Michael took Ariel's hand and muttered to her: "Here they come, I suppose they were always going to catch up with us."

She kissed him. "We'll keep away from them and mind our own business. We've come too far now for them; they can't touch us."

Jesus straightened up and called out to them: "The web is already upon you, if you look." He turned to Ariel and added succinctly: "There is no way of separating yourself from other men's business when they make it their business to include you in theirs. Two of these fellows come with good intentions but the third is a darkling thrush. He flatters himself with his struggle; he thinks himself a man of words and learning and he pins honors to his own chest. But he fights for nothing. He fights for the hollowed air where his body stands. He is a mere skin held up by his gaseous existence."

Ariel looked up. "Will you heal him?"

"If he asks to be healed… he will be healed."

43.

Giacomo and Paolo were shown to a vacant hut, where they put their packs down at the foot of the bunks and rested their aching limbs. Only Günter was unaffected by the long hike through the mountains. He sat in the doorway, looking with interest at the bustling settlement all about them: the carts passing by, the donkeys and goats, the digging of drainage ditches and laying of pipes, groups of elderly women on wooden chairs in the thoroughfares carding wool or embroidering cloth. Most of the men and some of the women were down in the valley on the fields, while gangs of carpenters put up more huts farther down the hill.

Steady streams of people were arriving all the time, carrying their belongings on their backs. Before long, this hilltop would be a town and, within a few years, a walled city.

Giacomo lay on his back, reading out aloud from Dr. Brunton's *The Spiritual Crisis of Man*. "Listen to this," he said: "'The human entity's inordinate clinging to its combative animality and selfish personality is being challenged and attacked by world forces and turned into a cause of its own psychic suffering...' What are these supposed world forces, then?" He yawned.

Günter turned round in the doorway. "The Devil, you dumb shit. And by this I mean the absence of anything worthwhile, which quickly grows a nose, eyes, and ears. The Devil is just a name we give it."

"Günter, do me a favor," said Giacomo. "Make yourself scarce. Go lay a cable or something."

"Some people shouldn't read books. It goes to their heads."

The three friends lay down and rested, each of them seething in his own, private universe.

Giacomo, because he considered his thoughts to be undervalued by the others.

Paolo, because his longing for prayer was always disrupted by his clannish need of friendship.

And Günter, because he viewed most humans as puffed-up idiots concerned with nothing more than the outward forms of things and plagued by hypocrisy.

A fine mist of unspoken conflict settled over them.

Finally Giacomo spoke: "In a while we'll go and introduce ourselves to… well, you know who I mean."

"He means Jesus, but he can't say it," said Günter.

Sleep was most welcome. Outside, the birds seemed to be twittering, full of well-being, nothing much concerning them beyond the occasional pecking at seeds or sitting on branches puffing their feathers.

After a few hours of pleasant repose, the two men and the dog (rolled up on the floor) began to stir and stretch their aching limbs.

"Two things occur to me," said Giacomo, the old spark in his eye returning. "First, I want to eat. Then I'll go and have a look at…"—he glared at Günter—"…Jesus."

"In that order, you miserable old glutton," said Paolo, with guilty delight. "You forget we haven't any food."

"Ah, how wrong he is. I bought a piece of smoked meat in the valley," said Giacomo proudly, "and a skin of wine." He rummaged in his pack and placed his treasures on a flat stone, sniffing the meat with deep relish. "Mutton is undervalued, particularly when smoked."

"What about oil and bread?" said Paolo.

"Oil, yes, but no bread, only a small bag of flour. Have no fear, Paolo. Before nightfall you shall have bread and meat and enough wine to stir your mind into repose."

"To stir my mind into repose? What a very odd thing to say, my old friend. Repose comes very easily to me," said Paolo, patting Giacomo's shoulder. "Are you sure you're all right?"

"Oh, I'm fine. A little nervous at the prospect of meeting our Redeemer, I'll confess. The life of a priest is all preparation, but we don't expect to come face to face with Him before our time is due."

His ruminations were disturbed by Günter shaking his head and flapping his fleshy lips. "Bread is for pot-bellied men, in fact men very much like you. Give me meat to make my muscles hard. And water to settle my mind. Let's get on with it."

They made a campfire. As dusk set in, they squatted on the ground and stared into the dancing flames. Giacomo baked on a flatiron he'd brought expressly for that purpose, lugging it over the sharp peaks of the Pyrenees, all for his faithful love of wheat.

After they'd luxuriated another hour, digesting, they set up the hill to find Jesus.

The huts had proliferated in higgledy-piggledy fashion. There was no system to it, no street names. Everywhere sat tired laborers with their families, eating or sleeping in their doorways by glowing embers or clay ovens.

At the top of the hill they found the camper bus, beside what they assumed to be a chapel. Yet it had no belfry, no crucifixes, no stained-glass windows, and was no more than a simple wattle-and-daub shelter with a thatched roof. A rectangle of hard, tanned calf leather served for a door. Hesitantly they pushed it aside and called out before entering.

On the floor, wrapped in a sheepskin, lay a woman with a baby at her breast.

Giacomo drew himself up. "Excuse us, young woman," he said. "We are looking for Jesus."

The woman tore her eyes away from her child, her lips curled with maternal tenderness. Her face was graceful, with the high cheekbones, dusky skin, and aquiline nose of an Ethiopian. "Everyone looks for him," she said. "He cannot be found."

She plucked the child away from her nipple and closed her tunic.

"Where is he?" Giacomo piped.

"At night he goes into the mountains."

"And in the day?"

"In the day he's sometimes here and sometimes in the fields."

Giacomo drew nearer, keeping his eyes on her. "And who might you be?"

Her white, well-shaped teeth glittered in the dark. "I knew him two thousand years ago, and I loved him then as I do now. Who I am is not very important."

Giacomo stood rocking to and fro, staring fiercely at her as she sat up, wrapping her child in swaddling.

"We'll be back tomorrow; tell your husband... if husband he is... that we'd like a word with him," he said on his way out of the chapel.

Paolo and Günter followed him outside with loud groans and sighs. As they emerged they found him hyperventilating and swearing.

"This is exactly what I thought would happen!" he roared as he led them down the hill. "Rank heresy of the first order. The man who led these people here is not Jesus at all. This supposed child of his cannot possibly be his child, can't you two idiots see that? Jesus is a maggot—any child of his would be a biological impossibility!"

As they descended the hill they saw a procession moving towards them, lit up by torches. At the front, Giacomo saw a tall, lean man surrounded by plowmen and farmhands.

The procession stopped directly ahead of them.

Jesus stood there gazing at them.

"My Lord." Paolo kneeled, his knees apparently lubricated.

Günter was also submissive, but it was harder for a dog to pay its respects. In his general excitement he forgot to stop wagging his tail.

Jesus immediately walked up to Günter and stroked his head. "Who is this brave man," he asked, "maltreated by his brothers and sisters?"

Next, Jesus looked at Paolo and touched his forehead. "Welcome, brother, at our table."

But when he turned to face Giacomo, Jesus's voice changed. It dropped an octave and there was almost something conspiratorial in the way he addressed him: "So, the orator has come, but we shall not listen to his long-winded songs." He leaned forward and whispered into Giacomo's ear: "You must die, my friend; die. Only then will I welcome you."

44.

Giacomo spent the next few weeks in shock, sitting in an upholstered chair which he placed in the middle of a verdant patch of ground at the foot of Jesus's hill, with a lovely view of clumps of flowering hazelnut and willow trees studding the banks of the stream. Come rain or shine, he sat in his chair, not caring that it was ripped, sodden, and crawling with insects, the lining spilling out like a white beard.

He stopped shaving, stopped combing his hair. He even stopped washing his tubby body, so that by and by the always slightly disheveled, food-stained Abbot turned into a bit of a spectacle whose odor hung disreputably about him.

When his friends asked what he was doing there, he answered:

"I am looking at the flowers, the clouds, the hills, the river. I need to take time to give myself time. I am doubly removed from contemplation, first by my humanity and secondly by my maggothood."

His words were complex, and people assumed he knew something they did not.

Paolo had joined Jesus's entourage. He was usually absent, and whenever he turned up to visit Giacomo, he was bursting with joy like a swelling droplet hanging from a petal.

Günter, on the other hand, spent most of his time lying in the deep bracken under the trees, or rolling on his back among the wild thyme and sprouting *ruccola*. He inhaled these fragrances with delight. For Günter this was a time of upheaval, not least physiologically. Since their arrival, a pair of tiny feet had started forming under the skin of his groin. Within a week or two the pink toes were pushing through the skin, itching slightly. As they grew, the shins followed, then the knees and thighs, although two hairy hind legs still hung from his hips like appendages fit for a monster of a traveling circus.

"You know the body is all we've got. We think with our bodies, we exist through our bodies, and right now I've got six damned legs, two of them about as useful as spare assholes."

Looking at him, one could not be sure what he was: a man wearing a dog's pelt on his back or some freakish werewolf? And so he kept out of view, ashamed of himself. He still loved to roll on his back like the dog he was, exclaiming as he did so with his great tongue lolling:

"I'll miss it, you know, the hairiness and robustness of a dog's body, its stamina, the strength of these teeth I can crack bones with. Humans are bloody pussy willows, aren't they? Besides, what human being can lie naked on his back like this, rolling his balls around without a care in the world?"

Giacomo listened to Günter absentmindedly, his mind at this time steeped in remembrance of his many years on this Earth. The only good thing that had happened to him was that his memory had come back. Childhood was a very distant pocket of light still illuminating his life with a slightly eerie and preternatural intensity—although Giacomo suspected it was mostly invented. He also recalled the early years, a time of weighty illusions, foolishness, and self-aggrandizement. This had been followed by maturity, a smug era of self-approval. Then his middle years, bursting with denial, confusion, and justifications. Now, at last, like an old mushroom in the forest, he had come to the moment when he must drop his spores.

"I wonder if I'm a toxic mushroom?" he asked himself, suspecting that he probably was a very toxic one.

Günter, always a great observer, liked to lie at Giacomo's feet watching the old man's emotions passing over his face like clouds.

"And I also wonder," said Giacomo with some sadness, "whether anyone likes me. I mean anyone at all." He looked at his friend. "Do you like me, for instance?"

"I don't really like people very much; they're just blobs moving about, getting in your face," said Günter, who was good at white lies.

About three months into their self-imposed seclusion, Günter was still spending his days with Giacomo, occasionally trying his weight on his brand new human legs or shaking the mangy pelt on his lower back like a diabolical cloak grown into his upper body.

Once he'd shed his canine skin and was able to look at his reflection in the river without shuddering at his ugliness, he took his farewell of the old man.

"Why don't you come, Giacomo? Come to the city with me."

Giacomo took a long time to answer, keeping his eyes on the lush river meadows. "I've decided I'm going to spend the rest of my life here, on this hill, looking at the trees and the river," he said. "I'm going to have a house built in the meadow. A group of builders and tradesmen will come very soon from Rome to put up a priory here. Then I'll make a garden with a good carp pond and a dovecote. I'll recreate the lives of the ancient monks. I'll spend my time in prayer." He sighed. "And when the time is right I'll have myself emptied and buried here with instructions that I'm not to be woken for at least a thousand years."

"Somehow I don't really think it works like that anymore," said Günter. "Just look at what's happened to me. I'm turning into a man again. Soon these old hind legs of mine will fall off like shriveled twigs. I'll have to look in the mirror and see whether I'm a Günter, a James, a Matthew, or just plain old Fred. What I mean is there aren't any maggot people anymore.

We can't go swinishly through the centuries like pigs in clover. We have to face the music."

Giacomo sat for a long while listening to the tinkle of the stream, the meandering wind in the treetops stirring the leaves, and the crows caw-cawing as they had always done, frustrated at their lack of vocabulary.

"Do you know this?" he said.

"Everyone knows it."

Giacomo smiled bitterly. From somewhere in the depths of a dream, he seemed to hear the unmistakable sound of masonry collapsing.

He took a pocket knife and scored a deep cut in his thumb. At first there was nothing apart from a sharp pain. Then a slow trickle of blood, like water rising in a once-dry well.

Giacomo had not seen his own blood for more than a thousand years.

45.

Not many weeks after, Michael and Ariel were sitting by a hearth watching Jesus expertly tossing flatbread onto the embers of the fire. His hands moved swiftly, turning the bread without scorching himself and then passing it to those sitting beside him.

His wife was breastfeeding their child.

"Now you eat," she said.

"I am not hungry," said Jesus, who had spent all day cutting brushwood. His face looked drawn and preoccupied.

Ariel drenched the bread in oil and topped it with fresh white cheese, honey and parsley. She was ravenous; she had grown heavy and was accustomed to the sensation of little feet drumming inside her womb.

A somber feeling hung over their little group. Jesus turned his amber eyes on them:

"We are leaving. You know this," he said. "You all have journeys you must make. We also have our journey."

"But why? And where will you go?" said Ariel.

"You shouldn't be so concerned with where," said Jesus. "It is a great irrelevance, of interest only to those caught in the comings and goings, the hither and thither of things. We will go where we must go. What more could anyone do?"

"We will do the same," said Michael. "But we don't know where?"

"Good," said Jesus. He turned to his wife and for a moment, his eyes filled with something like human warmth. She threw a few sprigs of dried sage on the fire and wafted the fragrant smoke towards them.

The moment was only slightly marred by the sound of metallic hammering, chisels against stone, from the bottom of the valley. Just about visible over the tree tops below was a substantial roof and a number of tall brick chimneys, growing taller by the day.

Their thoughts turned to this emanation of stone—Giacomo's house.

"What can be done about the visitor who comes uninvited and will not leave?" asked Michael.

"One must share equally with him," said Jesus. "Soon there will also be soldiers and priests and bishops arriving. They will all say they're here for our benefit." He smiled. "But they will find my name much more useful once I'm no longer here. Many witnesses will come forward. They will quote from the book, although there is no book."

The din from down below had first begun with the arrival of a rabble of laborers from the Vatican, laborers who had cleared a large area of trees, then set about laying down foundations, including large vaulted cellars and staircases. Carts drawn by oxen had brought fine cut stone, now slowly and artfully being turned into a palatial dwelling. Ducts and cisterns for water and sewerage had already been sunk into the ground, leading into underground chambers and shafts. A deep, stone-lined well had also been dug, and an eel released to live out its solitary life inside the stone drum, as was customary.

At the edge of the construction site were large tents which, in addition to the laborers, housed a group of Vatican soldiers, whose horses now also cropped the outlying fields.

At night, one smelled lamb roasting on their fires. Shepherds had been engaged, shepherds whose flocks littered the upper slopes by day.

Vatican officials had also had a substantial gate built at the base of the hill, with a low-lying but solid granite wall. Meanwhile at the far end of the valley, teams of workers were building a road in the Roman style, digging ditches and laying down beds of gravel topped by good-quality dressed granite from Norway. One day soon a horse-drawn carriage would be able to make good speed between the Vatican and the City of God, entering through the massive carved gate patrolled at night by sentinels.

The pope himself would be able to come and sleep on linen sheets in airy rooms. In the mornings he would feast on dove eggs and smoked trout, while in the outhouses vats of beer farted gently as the yeast and hops bubbled, or wine rested in oaken barrels in the cellars below.

Plans were under way for a new cathedral. Donations were flooding in from rich merchants. Bands of architects and builders had already formed themselves into mystical guilds. Without computers and hydraulics, they had returned to pencil and rule and algebra. Their craft was once again steeped in Masonic obscurity.

Giacomo had still not moved from his chair. His beard had now reached his waist, and his clothes were practically falling off his body. Seamstresses sewed patches on his tunic to keep him modest, and sometimes at night he was undressed and washed, and his linen cleaned. The bandy-legged old man—for since his return to flesh and blood he'd aged rapidly—was kept alive on a diet of fish and fruit. All the weight had fallen off him; his face looked suitably emaciated, and those eyes of his, once so lively and malicious, now stared tetchily at anyone who spoke to him.

Deep down, Giacomo knew that his pride kept him where he was. He had not seen Jesus since that encounter on the mountain. The mere mention of his name brought his hands out in livid stigmata.

The humiliation of seeing how worthless his life had been, in spite of his thousand-year spell, gnawed at him.

He asked himself: What do I still have before me in this life?

And the answer was *nothing*.

But to everyone else who saw him, Giacomo seemed the very essence of holiness and as soon as the palace was ready they carried him into the grandest, most beautiful room, where he spent the rest of his life in silence.

A century later, when the cathedral was completed, his chair was placed in a glass case. And his miraculously reconstituted bones were smoothed by the doting hands of throngs of pilgrims who came to pray by St. Giacomo's Shrine.